THE SEARCH FOR SOMETHING GREATER

God Bless!

Jenniffer Clark

Jenniffer Clark

Fulton Books
Meadville, PA

Published by Fulton Books 2023

ISBN 979-8-88982-291-2 (paperback)
ISBN 979-8-88982-292-9 (digital)

Printed in the United States of America

I t was my seventh birthday, and my parents wanted to take me out for ice cream. I was already in my pajamas, so when we pulled up to the twenty-four-hour ice cream parlor, they told me to lock the doors and stay in the car. I could remember it like it was yesterday. They walked quickly into the parlor, and that was the last time I saw my parents. I must have fallen asleep waiting for them to come back because the next thing I remembered was a cop knocking on the car window to get my attention.

"What are you doing alone in the middle of the night?" the officer asked as I opened the door for him.

"My parents ran into the ice cream parlor to get me some birthday ice cream, and they told me to wait here," I replied, starting to cry.

"Okay, okay! Don't cry. Let's go try and find them." The officer helped me out of the car and took my hand as we headed into the parlor.

When we got into the parlor, the guy at the counter said they had left about three hours ago. He informed the cop he did not know where they had gone.

"Let's get you that birthday ice cream and go back to my office." The officer grinned as he lifted me up to see the ice cream flavors.

When we got to the police station, the officer made me a place on the floor to sleep.

He never found my parents, and I ended up going to a foster home. I was in ten different foster families over the next nine years. I was always treated like an outsider. They only wanted me around so that they could get money from the government and so that I could take care of their children while they got drunk. I never had a real family who loved me and treated me like I was a person. My caseworker just called me and told me that he is coming to pick me up so that he can take me to my new foster family because the family I am with kicked me out because I would not go buy them more alcohol. I hope the family I am going to does not drink.

"So, Shane, where am I off to this time?" I asked as we began to drive out of Kansas.

"Well, Rose, you see, I have a friend who works in Delaware County in Oklahoma, and she found a family who wants you to come live with them. However, this means I will no longer be your caseworker. I will be turning you over to Susan. You will love her. Do not worry," he explained as we drove toward Oklahoma.

"You mean I will never see you again?" I did not want to lose everyone I knew. Everything was slipping away so fast.

"You can still call me or visit any time you want, and I will come visit you from time to time," Shane replied as he flashed his warm smile at me.

After a few hours, he pulled up to a very pretty house in the middle of a very small town. Standing in the front yard was a beautiful lady who seemed to be waiting for us.

"Is that the mom?" I asked Shane as we got out of the car.

"No, that is Susan, your new caseworker," Shane explained as we got closer to Susan.

"Hi, Shane, how are you? This must be Rose? It is a pleasure to meet you, Rose," Susan greeted us.

"Hi, Susan, it's nice to meet you as well," I politely replied.

"Hi, Susan, here are Rose's files and information. I hope this helps you with a smooth transition," Shane expressed with a smile.

"Great, thank you so much. Are you ready to meet your new family?" Susan asked as she motioned us to the door.

"As ready as I will ever be, I guess," I answered as I walked up to the house.

The house was a two-story antique-looking house. It had a wraparound porch that was made out of beautiful oak wood. As we approached the house, we were greeted with three steps leading up to an amazing set of French doors that had a painting of a cross in the glass. As we climbed the three steps, a couple opened the French doors.

"Hello, you must be Rose. We are so blessed to welcome you into our home. My name is Leon, and this is my lovely wife, Irene. Please come in, come in." Leon smiled as we walked through the doors.

They were so nice to us; however, all I could think of was that this was how they all started out acting until Shane left. Why would they be any different? I studied them very carefully. Leon was a fairly tall man. He had brown hair and blue eyes. Irene was a few inches shorter than Leon with light-brown hair and green eyes. They were both fit people who appeared to work out regularly. I could tell that my strawberry-blonde hair and blue eyes would stand out. I was taller than Irene but not as tall as Leon. I felt uneasy because I felt that I was a lot bigger than both of them. I wore a size twenty, and Irene looked like she could fit into a size two. I felt like they were going to yell at me for being overweight after Shane left or just make fun of me for being fat.

"Can I get you a drink?" Irene asked us, interrupting my thoughts.

"Yes, please," I replied, rejoining the group.

"I will pass, thanks. I have to get back on the road and head toward the home front," Shane replied as he stood up.

I stood up and walked him out. We said our goodbyes, and I dragged myself back inside, ready for everything to turn into a nightmare.

"Well, it was a pleasure to meet you, Rose, and I will see you in my office in a week to see how everything is working out. If you need anything before then, here is my card. Feel free to call me anytime." Susan met me on her way out when I walked in the door.

"So would you like to see the rest of the house before settling in?" Irene asked as I rejoined them in the living room.

"Sure, I would like that," I replied, a little puzzled.

This was the first family who had been nice to me after Shane was gone. Usually, they told me to go to my room and not to bother them for any reason. That was usually the most conversation I had had with any of my foster parents unless they were yelling at me.

"Is everything okay, Rose?" Leon asked as they got up to walk out of the room. He must have seen the confusion on my face.

"I was just trying to figure out why you were being nice to me. I have never had a family show me kindness in the nine years of foster care." I went on to explain what I had encountered at my previous homes. I saw the sadness came over their faces. At that moment, I realized this was going to be a different kind of family.

"Rose, we want you here, and that will never change. You can talk to us about anything. We want you to feel like we are your family. On that note, are you ready to see your new house?" Leon explained as Irene took my arm and smiled.

"Thank you, that means a lot to me. Yes, I am ready to see the house." I smiled and walked out of the living room with them.

The house was amazing! We left the living room and walked into the formal dining room area where they had a beautiful dining set. After the dining room, we went into the kitchen where they had an island in the middle and a bar going around the kitchen in a U shape.

"Now while we are in here, I want you to know that you can help yourself to anything that is in the kitchen at all times. I grocery shop usually once a week, so if there is anything that you want, just write it on the little pad on the fridge, and I will be happy to get it for you," Irene explained as she showed me where some things were at in the cabinets.

After the kitchen, they showed me where the guest bedroom was and where their bedroom was located. After the bedrooms, they showed me the laundry room.

"Now we share the responsibilities of washing clothes. You have a hamper in your room, and it is your responsibility to bring your dirty clothes to the washroom. I normally do the laundry, but if there is a time when you bring your laundry down and there are a lot of dirty clothes, please start a load to help out," Irene politely explained.

"Okay, I can do that," I replied as we headed to the stairs that were beside the kitchen.

"The last thing on our stop is your room. Now it is not a lot because we wanted you to be able to decorate however you want, so Irene will take you shopping before you start school, and we will get whatever you want," Leon explained as we climbed the stairs.

As we walked up the stairs, I never dreamed that what I was about to see was all mine. The floor was like its own apartment. It had its own small kitchen area with a table that would seat two people. It had a medium-sized refrigerator and a two-burner stove. Beside the refrigerator, there was a sink and a cabinet under and above the sink. On the other side of the room was a bathroom. Inside the bathroom was a jet tub with a shower and a sink with a medicine cabinet above it and cabinets under it. The walk-in closet was also in the bathroom with another door leading out into the bedroom. The room had a king-sized bed on one wall, and the other half of the room was made up as a living room. It had a couch and a big-screen TV. It was the most amazing thing I had ever seen.

"Do you like it?" Leon asked as he handed me the keys.

"I...I love it," I replied in amazement.

"That door there leads outside to the pool and the hot tub. You can also use it to leave the house. We just ask that you let us know where you are going before you leave," Leon explained.

"This is amazing. Thank you," I expressed enthusiastically.

"I am so glad you like it." Irene smiled with excitement.

"Okay, Rose, we will leave you to get settled in. Dinner will be in an hour. We will discuss some house rules then. Just relax. This is your home now," Leon explained as they walked to the door.

They left, and I began unpacking. I did not have a lot of belongings, so it did not take me long to unpack. When I finished unpacking, I went downstairs to explore the house.

An hour passed, and it was finally time for dinner. I was worried about the rules they were getting ready to set. They had been so nice up to this point; it could all change in a split second.

"Okay, Rose, I know that you have had bad relationships with your previous foster parents, and we just want to let you know that this time will be different," Irene began to explain as we sat down to the table to start dinner.

"However, there are some ground rules that we need to make sure you understand. The first rule is that you have a ten o'clock curfew on school nights and twelve o'clock on weekends. The second one is we want to let you know that if you ever get into a situation with alcohol or drugs, call and we will come get you. This does not mean there will not be consequences. However, if you call, they will be less severe. Are you good so far?" Leon asked as he paused.

"Yes, I understand," I confirmed.

"Okay, then, lets continue. The third rule, we know you have your own door. However, we would appreciate you leaving a note or telling us where you are going. The fourth rule, you will have a few chores around the house, like cleaning your room and doing the dishes, and then each week, you will get an allowance. The last thing we want to talk about is that we are here to talk. We want you to talk to us about anything that comes to mind. Okay, those are all of the rules. Do you have any questions?" Leon asked, looking for my input.

"Oh, yes, we will go to church tomorrow, and you can meet some new kids your age," Irene chimed in happily.

"Okay, what do you do at church?" I had never been to church before.

"We will listen to a guy preach, we will sing, and then we are having dinner this Sunday. The dinners are only once in a while. You will enjoy it," Irene explained as we finished up dessert and cleared the table.

My alarm woke me up around seven-thirty Sunday morning. I was excited to go to church and try something new. I took a shower and started fixing my hair when I heard a knock on the door.

"Come in," I yelled from my bathroom.

"Good morning, Rose, I thought you might need a dress to wear to church," Irene entered, holding a red summer dress that was beautiful.

"Oh, I could not accept that." I had never had anything given to me.

"This is what family does, and you are in this family now, and we will buy you anything you need and even things you do not need." Irene smiled and squeezed my shoulder.

"Thank you very much. I am just not use to people being nice to me." I smiled as I hung the dress on the back of the door.

"Well, you will get used to it. We will leave at nine-thirty for church," Irene informed me as she closed the door behind her.

At nine-fifteen, I walked downstairs and met Irene and Leon in the kitchen. I grabbed a bagel, and we headed off to church.

As we pulled into the parking lot, I saw a beautiful building with stained-glass windows and big, wooden double doors. It was the most amazing thing I had ever seen. We got out and headed toward the front door of this beautiful building. As soon as we got in the door, people were shaking our hands and greeting us. I had never been in a place where so many people were friendly to everyone.

"Hi, I'm Sarah. You must be Rose. It is very nice to meet you." I heard a girl screeched from behind me as we started to sit down in a pew toward the back of the church.

"Oh, this is one of the girls that Irene was telling you about last night," Leon informed me as I turned around to meet her.

"Yes, I am Rose! It is nice to meet you as well," I replied with a smile.

"We are going to be great friends," Sarah exclaimed as we all took our seats, and a guy started speaking.

As soon as church was over, Sarah grabbed my arm and dragged me with her to the kitchen.

"We are so excited that we get to have a new friend in our group. Garrett had to miss today, but you can meet him tomorrow at school." Sarah handed me a plate as she continued to talk.

After lunch, I had learned that Sarah and Garrett were both juniors like me, and we had all the same classes. She told me all about her and Garrett. Garrett was Sarah's best friend. She spent an hour talking about what they did and what they liked before Irene came and got me to introduce me to some people in the church.

"I want to introduce you to the pastor and his family," Leon explained as he caught up to Irene and me.

"Now the pastor is the guy who was preaching, right?" I asked just to make sure I had the right guy.

"Rose, this is Gene and his wife, Melinda," Leon announced as we approached the table they were sitting at.

"It is nice to meet you, Rose. This is our daughter, Kylee." Melinda smiled as she pointed to the little girl sitting next to her.

"It is very nice to meet you all," I replied as I shook Gene's hand.

After talking with them for a few minutes and making plans to have dinner at our house Friday night to get to know one another, I made my way back to the table where Sarah was sitting. Along the way, I met many of the church members. They were all very friendly.

"Are you ready to go, Rose?" Irene asked me later.

"Yeah, I am ready," I replied as I turned to Sarah. "It was nice to meet you. I will see you tomorrow at school."

"Okay, I will see you then," Sarah replied, then we walked away.

"I thought we would drop Leon off at home, and then we would go clothes shopping and school supply shopping. What do you think?" Irene asked as we pulled out of the church parking lot.

"That sounds like fun. Are you sure you want to buy me more stuff?" I asked, concerned.

"Rose, you are a part of this family now, and you need to remember that. We want you here, and we want you to feel free to ask for anything you need or may want. We are here to support you," Irene responded to my question with love and security.

"Sorry, I am trying to get use to that idea. I will someday." I smiled.

"I think we will go to the mall to shop. We can get food there as well for dinner." Irene returned my smile as she explained where we would go.

"Okay, Leon, we will see you in a while. I will call you when we head home," Irene assured Leon, followed by a kiss, and we headed out the door.

"You, girls, have fun. I will see you later," he replied as he shut the front door.

We pulled up to this two-story building that was surrounded by a garden. Walking up the few stairs that led to the revolving glass doors, I was in awe. Inside it was amazing. There were stores all around us. In the middle of the room, there was a huge water fountain. People were sitting around it and talking. They had escalators to either side of us, and they also had a glass elevator close to the fountain so you could see the mall as you went up. It was a sight I had never seen before.

I could not believe the fun I was having. I got a new bag and supplies (both for home and school); I got a whole new wardrobe and new makeup. Irene insisted on me getting a new purse and even some decorations for my walls at home. I had never been able to wear makeup because no one would buy it for me. I believe that was about to change. Irene wanted to teach me all about makeup, and she even got me a new blow-dryer, curling iron, and a flatiron.

We went up to the second floor to find the food court and get some dinner. When I stepped off the elevator, I could not believe what I saw. There were twenty different fast-food places and one sit-down restaurant.

"Where would you like to eat, Rose?" Irene asked as we looked around.

"There are so many different places to choose from. What is Cheddar's?" I asked as I looked at the sign.

"You have never eaten at Cheddar's? Okay, we need to eat there. You will love it," Irene assured me as we headed toward the door.

"Order whatever you want, Rose. Do not worry about the price," Irene explained to Rose.

After we finished eating, we decided to head home.

"Thank you so much, Irene, for everything today. I have never had so much fun before." I was glowing with excitement.

"I am so glad to hear you enjoyed it," Irene exclaimed. It broke her heart to hear how I never got to do things like this before.

"Okay, Rose, here is the last of it. I will let you get everything put away like you want it. Just let us know if you need anything," Irene explained as she put down the last batch of sacks.

"Thank you so much, Irene," I replied with an ear-to-ear smile.

"Your welcome. Anytime." Irene smiled and closed the door.

"I am finished putting everything away, and now I think I will go on to bed," I told Irene and Leon as I walked into the living room where they were reading.

"Okay, dear, we will see you for breakfast at seven o'clock in the morning," Leon replied, standing to give me a hug. Irene was right behind with another hug.

My alarm went off at six o'clock in the morning, and I was dreading the first day at a new school. I had been to so many new schools, and I was always the outcast. I was the foster kid no one wanted. As soon as I made a friend, I would have to move. I got out of bed, took a shower, and enjoyed using all the new items I had gotten at the mall. I grabbed my bag and headed down to eat. I thought it would be cereal and that I would be eating alone; however, the Thomases just kept surprising me. I came down to a full breakfast on the table and everyone getting ready to eat together.

"Good morning," I expressed, trying to hold back my surprise.

"Good morning," they both replied as we all sat down for breakfast.

"Okay, so I will bring you to school today, and Leon will pick you up after school," Irene explained as she passed the pancakes.

"Sounds good to me," I replied.

"Oh, and one more thing you might need, this way, you can get peoples' numbers, and in case you need us, our numbers are in there." Leon handed me a new cell phone and showed me how to enter a contact.

"Wow, thank you so much," I exclaimed.

"You ready to go, Rose?" Irene asked as she put on her jacket and grabbed her purse.

"I am ready," I replied as I appeared out of the kitchen with my coat on, my backpack, and purse in hand.

When we arrived at the school, I could not believe what I saw. Sarah was standing outside, waiting for me. She was standing with a taller boy with short blonde hair and blue eyes and who was very good-looking. *It must be Garrett*, I thought.

"Have a great day and call if you need anything." Irene smiled as I opened the door and stepped out.

"See what I tell you, Garrett. She is hot," Sarah exclaimed before I made it to them.

"You were right. She is very attractive. I love that outfit," Garrett replied as he watched me walk to them. I was wearing black dress pants with a red dressy shirt on and black boots.

"Hi, Sarah, and you must be Garrett. I am Rose," I announced as I reached the two of them.

"Nice to meet you, Rose," Garrett acknowledged, shaking my hand.

"Are you ready for class? We all have the same schedule, so we can show you around." Garrett smiled and opened the door for us.

As we walked to our first class together, we got to know one another better.

Our first class was chemistry. It was the second semester of school, so everyone already had a partner for class except me; however, Garrett's partner was out sick, so I was partnered with Garrett. I was so excited that I would get to work closely with Garrett.

Next, we had English, Spanish, FACS, and, finally, lunch.

After lunch, we had algebra II, history, and study hall last period.

During lunch, we talked about what the teachers were like and just got to know one another better.

"Hey, Rose, do you want to ride to school with us tomorrow? We could pick you up on our way," Sarah asked.

"I would love to. I will have to make sure it is okay first. Can I get your number and call you guys tonight?" I asked.

"Yeah, that would be great," Garrett chimed in.

We exchanged phone numbers just in time for the bell to ring, and we headed off to class.

At the end of the day, I walked out of the school with Sarah and Garrett where they departed, and I met Leon at the parking lot.

"So how was your first day of school?" he asked as he started backing out of the parking space.

"It was a lot of fun. I learned a lot of new things," I explained as we drove home.

At supper, I went into great detail all about what happened at school.

"Would you mind if I rode to school with Sarah and Garrett tomorrow?" I asked as we cleaned the table off from dinner.

"Not at all. That would be just fine with us," Irene nearly blurted with excitement.

"Thank you! I am going to call them and let them know." I skipped up to my room.

"Hello?"

"Hey, Garrett."

"Hey, Rose, what's up?"

"I just wanted to let you know that it is okay if you still want to come pick me up tomorrow."

"Okay, that is great. We will be there around seven-thirty to get you then."

"Sounds good. I will see you then."

"Okay, good night, Rose."

"Good night, Garrett."

The rest of the week was similar to my first day. Garrett picked me up every morning and brought me home after school.

On Thursday, we got assigned a huge history group project. Garrett, Sarah, and I all got in the same group. The assignment was to write a report on one aspect of our founding fathers.

"Do you guys want to work on the project this weekend?" Sarah asked on the way to my house.

"I can on Saturday or after church on Sunday," I explained.

"Saturday is good with me," Garrett agreed.

"Great, we will work on it Saturday." Sarah was excited; she loved schoolwork.

On Friday, when I got home from school, I found my mom, which I started calling Irene, getting ready for the dinner party that I had forgotten all about.

"Oh, good, your home. Would you mind helping me?" Irene asked when she saw me.

"No problem. Let me just put my stuff up," I replied, running upstairs to put my bag up. Then I returned to the kitchen to set the table.

We finished getting all the food on the table when the doorbell rang. I went to the door to invite them in.

"Please come on in," I said, inviting them in, and as the last person walked through the door, my heart dropped.

"Hi, Rose," the familiar face greeted me.

"Garrett?" I said, not understanding.

"Garrett is our son. He was not at church last Sunday for us to introduce him to you," Gene explained.

"Oh, I see." I smiled and shut the door behind him. "May I take your coats?" I asked, holding my arm out as Irene met us in the living room.

"Yes, thank you." Melinda smiled as she sat the baby down and took off her coat.

"I will help you." Garrett smiled as he took his dad's coat and followed me to the closet.

"So you're the preacher's son, huh?" I joked as we hung the coats up.

"Yeah, well, I try not to brag." He laughed.

"I am glad you are here, someone my own age." I smiled as we walked to the living room to rejoin the rest of the group.

"If everyone will follow me, supper is ready," Leon announced from the doorway.

As we sat down, Irene got everyone a drink. We talked all through dinner. We talked about school, church, family, and anything else we thought of. It felt good to be a part of a family dinner party.

At the end of the dinner, I volunteered to clear the table while everyone went into the living room to finish talking. Garrett stayed behind to help. I had never felt this way toward a guy before. Whenever he was around, my heart rose, and I felt like I was floating on clouds. I had friendships with boys before, but I had never had a boyfriend. Not that Garrett was a boyfriend. I had always just been one of the guys. I loved spending time with him. We joined the others in the living room just as they were standing to leave.

"It has been a pleasure, but we should really get Kylee home to bed now," Gene announced as he and Garrett went to get their coats.

"Thanks again for everything." Melinda smiled as she put her coat on and picked up her stuff.

"Thanks for coming. We will see you Sunday." Leon escorted them to the door.

"Rose, I will see you tomorrow. I will pick you up around ten. Is that okay?" Garrett asked before going out the door.

"That is great! I will see you then." I smiled and shut the door behind him.

"Wow, you already have a date with Garrett. That was fast. Way to go," Irene teased.

"What? No. We are just working on a school project with Sarah," I stuttered, embarrassed.

"I was just kidding, sweetie. It is good that you are hanging out with them," Irene assured me.

"Oh, okay. Thanks. I am going upstairs to do some homework," I let them know as I headed upstairs. I wanted to be ready for tomorrow even though we had not chosen a specific topic.

Garrett showed up a little after ten the next morning, and I was ready. I told my mom and dad "bye" and ran out to meet him.

"Good morning, Garrett."

"Good morning," he replied.

"Where is Sarah? I thought she was getting picked up first," I asked as I climbed into his truck.

"She cannot make it until around two this afternoon, so I told her to meet us at my house," he replied.

"Oh, well, we could have moved it until two," I said, not wanting to move it.

"We could have. However, I wanted to spend time with you, so I thought we could watch a movie and have lunch at my house before we start the project," Garrett replied with a huge smile.

I knew right then that my face was beet red, but I did not care. No one had ever wanted to spend time with me. I had a good feeling today would be a great day.

We talked a little on the way to his house; mainly, we sat in silence.

As we pulled into his driveway, he insisted on getting my door and carrying my backpack for me. He was a true gentleman.

"What movie would you like to watch?" Garrett asked as we walked into his living room, and I saw a huge collection of movies to choose from. There had to be at least three hundred movies.

"What is your favorite movie, Garrett?" I asked as I looked through the movies.

"I have tons of favorites. However, one of them is *Facing the Giants*. I feel it helps me get through each day. Have you ever seen it?" he asked as he handed me the movie.

"No, I haven't seen a lot of movies. It sounds good though, so let's watch it," I replied with a smile.

"Great, I'm gonna go get us some popcorn and drinks. I will be right back, so make yourself at home." Garrett was excited as he disappeared into the kitchen.

I found a comfortable spot on the couch and sat down and waited for him to return.

When he walked out of the kitchen, he had drinks, popcorn, and candy, just like we were in a real theater.

"Here is your Dr. Pepper, and I got you some Reese's Pieces. I hope you like them." Garrett handed me a small bag of candy.

"Thank you. I love them," I replied as he sat beside me.

The movie was a really good movie and helped me think about my own life. I knew that I was missing something in my life, and I had been trying so hard to fill it with all the wrong things. However, I didn't want to ruin the day by asking Garrett questions, so I decided it could wait.

After the movie was over, we went into the kitchen and had some sandwiches for lunch, and then we decided to start on the project.

"So do you have any ideas on what we could write about our founding fathers?" Garrett asked me as we settled down at the kitchen table.

"Well, I was reading last night, and something confused me. It talked about how our nation was founded on the Word of God, but now the government is trying to take God out of everything. Was religion really an important part of our founding fathers?"

"Yes, that is true, and in fact, that is a great subject to write about for class," Garrett said as he got up to get a book from his dad's office.

"Do you think our teacher will like that topic?" I asked when he returned.

"I do not see why not. It is actual facts, and that is all we will write. We will leave out personal opinions," Garrett explained.

"Okay, sounds good to me," I replied as I picked up the book he had sat on the table.

As we started getting the facts together, the doorbell rang, and in walked Sarah.

"Hey, group, how is the project going?" she asked as she joined us at the table.

"It is good. We have just picked the subject and are researching it. We decided to write about the faith of our founding fathers," Garrett filled her in and gave her a different book.

"Is that okay with you, Sarah?" I asked, not wanting to hurt her feelings.

"Sounds good to me. Let's get started."

We worked for hours before we finished getting all our research together. Then we decided to finish working on it after supper. We finished the project around eight, and Garrett took me home. I was sad to say "good night," but I knew I would see him tomorrow.

Sunday went by fast just like I figured it would because we had to present our assignment Monday at school. After church, we had some family game time, and it was a lot of fun. We played a bunch of different card games; some I knew, and some they had to teach me.

Monday, we decided to volunteer to go first with our presentation. We mainly just wanted to get it over with. I had never been very good at public speaking. Usually, I got away with just doing the research, and someone else did the speaking. However, this teacher said that every member had to speak to receive a grade. We had worked it out where each one of us had a specific assignment; however, Garrett was doing most of the talking. Our assignment was one of the most in-depth, and we received an A.

I had been with Irene and Leon for a week, and I had never felt this way before. Before I was placed with this family, I felt that I had emptiness in myself that I was sure was because I had never had a true family. I thought once I got here and started making friends, then the emptiness would go away. However, I was happy, but there was still a feeling of emptiness and loneliness. What could fill this emptiness inside me? Maybe after a while, I would find out.

It had been a month, and Thanksgiving was just a few weeks away.

In the last month, I had really settled in, and Garrett, Sarah, and I had become inseparable. I felt like this was truly home. This year, Thanksgiving had a whole new meaning to me.

"Hey, Rose, I was wondering if you could babysit Kylee Friday evening while Gene and I go to a diner with some church members?" Melinda asked as she stopped me after church on Sunday morning.

"I would love to. Is Garrett going with you?" I asked, wondering if he would be at the house.

"Yes, it is at Rachael's house, and she really wants him to come," she responded.

Rachael was the captain of the cheerleading squad and a very beautiful girl. She had made it abundantly clear that she wanted Garrett all to herself. She had warned me about getting too close to him.

"Okay, that is awesome. I will be there. What time do you need me?" I agreed even though I didn't like the fact that he would be spending the evening with Rachael. I finally thought that we could really have a chance because we were getting so close over the past month.

"How about 5:30 p.m.? I can have Garrett come get you if you would like?" Melinda asked, breaking me away from my thoughts.

"No, that is okay. I will have Mom bring me over. Thank you. I will see you then," I replied as I waved and headed to the parking lot to meet Mom and Dad.

"What did Melinda want?" Mom asked as I climbed in the car.

"She needs me to babysit on Friday. Is that all right?" I asked as I buckled.

"Oh, that is great. Just remember that we have a court date on Friday also, so you won't be in school," Dad reminded me.

Apparently, my real parents found me and thought they needed me back. It had been ten years since they left me at the ice cream parlor and never returned. I was sure they only wanted me to get money or something before I turned eighteen. I was seventeen, so I had to give my opinion and explain how I felt about the whole situation. I had no idea what I was going to say.

"Have you thought about what you want to tell the judge?" Mom interrupted my painful memories.

"I have been thinking about it. I just haven't come up with exactly what I want to say. I will work on it tomorrow after school," I explained.

"Okay, you have a few days, so take your time. This is important," Dad chimed in as we started pulling out of the parking lot.

The week went by so fast. It was Wednesday before I knew it, and I had not written what I wanted to say to the judge. There was so much I wanted to say. I didn't know how to word it.

That night, we had church, and then I had to start working on it.

At church, we had a Bible study and special guest speakers sometimes.

We got home, and after dinner, I went to my room to start writing my speech. I got the notebook ready and just started writing what was on my mind.

I remember the night my biological parents decided to take me to get ice cream for my birthday. I was seven, and I had already gotten ready for bed, so they told me to stay in the car and that they would run in and grab the ice cream and be right back out. After a while, a police officer woke me up and ended up taking me to the station, and I ended up in foster care. Every day after that, I have always wondered why my parents did not want me. I did not understand what I had done to make them leave me alone. Every time I had to switch foster homes, I felt like I had done something wrong. Now, after ten years, they come back into my life and think all is forgivable. I just don't see...

"Rose, it is ten o'clock. Are you ready for bed?" Mom asked as she walked into my room.

"Oh, I lost track of time. Sorry, I will get ready now." I jumped up and put the notebook in my backpack.

"Okay, sweetie, sweet dreams." Mom closed the door as I got dressed for bed.

The next morning, all I could think about was the speech I needed to finish. My morning classes were all a blur, and when lunchtime came, I decided not to eat. Instead, I found a classroom I could sit in to finish my speech. I usually ate lunch with Garrett and Sarah. However, I figured they would not miss me one day. I decided to start where I left off.

I just don't see how they expect me to be okay with them coming back into my life. This last month with the Thomases has been something I never thought I would ever be able to have. I found a family who does not just keep me around for the monthly checks. They care about me and show me every day how important I am to them. Not only do I feel like I finally have a family but I also have great friends. Garrett and Sarah have helped me finally enjoy going to school, and I make straight As. I feel like this is the best place for me. I think that sending me back to my real parents would be the wrong thing to do.

"Rose, what are you doing in here?" Garrett asked as he opened the classroom door.

"What! Oh, sorry, you startled me," I answered as I quickly put up the letter. I didn't want him to know what I was doing tomorrow. Even though Garrett and I had become really close, I had not told him about my history. All he knew was that I was a foster child who came to live with the Thomases.

"We got worried when you did not show up for lunch, so I decided to come find you," he explained with worry in his smile.

"Well, thanks for your concern. I just had to finish a paper, so I thought I would skip lunch today." I stood up and walked with him out into the hallway.

"Oh, okay. Well, I did not mean to make you quit what you were doing," Garrett said sadly.

"No, it is okay. I was pretty much done anyway," I replied. I figured I wasn't going to get it perfect anyways.

A few hours later, it was time to go home. Garrett and I walked to his truck, and we headed toward my house.

"Thanks for the ride, Garrett. I will not need a ride the rest of the week. I will not be at school. I have a few appointments. So if you wouldn't mind, please get any assignments I miss, and I will pick them up sometime this weekend," I explained as I got out of the car.

"Oh, okay. I will call you and let you know what you missed. Have a good weekend then," he replied.

"Thank you. You have a good weekend also." I smiled, knowing that the next two days were going to be very challenging. The judge had asked to see me the day before the court meeting so we could talk about everything.

I woke up Thursday morning with butterflies in my stomach. I had no idea how the judge would react to what I had to say. I printed off the letter I had typed last night, put on my nice clothes, and headed downstairs to meet Mom and Dad. They had both taken off work for the rest of the week to be with me.

"Are you ready for today?" Mom asked as I walked into the kitchen.

"Just remember, sweetie, that today is just you and the judge. We will not even be in the room. He just wants to talk to you a little before everyone is there tomorrow," Dad explained as we sat down for breakfast.

"I know. I am nervous and ready all at the same time. I want this to all be put behind me." I smiled and began eating.

"Okay, let's get going so we are not late," Mom said as she loaded the last dish in the dishwasher.

"Okay, let's do this." I grabbed my purse and headed out the door.

"Judge Barry is ready to see you now," the secretary said as she opened the office door.

"Okay, just be honest, and everything will be great. No matter what, we love you, and that will never change."

Mom and Dad both gave me a hug, and I headed into the judge's chambers.

"Hi, Rose, it is very nice to meet you. I am sorry that we are meeting under these circumstances." Judge Barry shook my hand and motioned for me to have a seat.

"It is very nice to meet you as well, Judge Barry," I replied as I sat down.

"Today, I want you to just tell me anything you want about how you feel in this whole situation. I don't care if it is good, bad, or indifferent. This time is for you to get whatever you want to say off your chest to help me in my decision. What you say today will not all be shared with everyone tomorrow. We will discuss what you need to talk about in court tomorrow after we talk."

Judge Barry was very nice and laid-back for our meeting. I felt very comfortable with him.

"Well, I wrote you a letter, so here is the letter."

I handed him the letter, and he quickly read over it.

"Okay, and anything else you want to add to it?" he asked as he sat beside me.

I figured I needed to share everything with him to have a better chance of staying with my new family, so I just let go.

"I do not understand why they left me for ten years and now decided to come back into my life and how they can honestly believe that the best thing for me is to go back with them. I'll turn eighteen in a little under a year, and how will they feel then? Will they just throw me out on the streets because they cannot get money for me anymore? My mom and dad (the Thomases) have already started talking about what college I might want to go to. Are my biological parents going to encourage me to go to college? Are they going to be able to help me pay for college like Mom and Dad can? I have so much going on in my head, and I just do not know what to think. I felt, for so long, that I was the reason they left and that there was something wrong with me. I did not stop feeling that until I moved in with the Thomases. They helped me understand that I am special, that they love me, that God always loves me and that he will never leave me and neither will they. I finally feel like I have a reason to be happy and to live because someone loves me and wants me as a part of their family. I do not hate my biological parents at all. I forgave them a long time ago. I just wish they cared enough to let me stay where I am."

I finally decided that was enough to put out on the table for now.

"I am very happy that you can be so honest with me. Tomorrow, just keep it at you do not understand why they left you, you felt, for so long, like you were worthless, you have grown to know someone can love you, and you are worth living. If you feel like you want to, you might even tell them that you forgive them for what they did and that you would like them to show you how much they care by letting you stay with the Thomases. Now that decision is ultimately up to me. However, I will take a recess after you speak to talk with your biological parents, and if they want to drop the case, that is what we will do. If they do decide to drop the case, would you like to speak with them before they leave? I can be with you if you would like just so you can say anything else you would like to them?"

"I understand, and yes, I would like to speak to them and tell them how much I love them and how I truly have forgave them and to thank them for what they are doing for me."

"Okay, then, we will see you at ten o'clock in the morning, and do not worry. Everything will turn out. Just keep your head up and trust that God will see you through."

"Thank you, Judge Barry, for everything. I feel better about tomorrow. I will see you then."

I turned and headed for the door.

"Oh, and, Rose, if you want to have your friends here for support, we will let anyone you want into the courtroom," Judge Barry added before I walked out.

"Thank you," I acknowledged as I walked out into the waiting area where my parents were waiting for me.

"Are you ready to go, sweetie?" Dad asked as he stood up to put his arm around me.

"Yes, let's go. I have to be back at ten o'clock in the morning," I replied as I picked up my purse from where my mom had sat it in the chair.

"Okay, let's go."

Mom stood up, and we walked out of the building.

"Hey, Mom and Dad, Judge Barry suggested that I ask my friends to come tomorrow for support. I do not want Garrett or Sarah to go, but I do think it would be good for someone to be there who will provide us with encouragement and support, so I was wondering if you could drop me off at Bro Gene's office so that I could see if he would be interested in going with us?" I explained as we climbed in the car and headed off.

"Yes, I think that is a great idea, Rose. We will drop you off, and then we can pick you up after we run some errands," Leon explained, turning toward the church.

"Okay, I will see you in a little while. It will take me a little bit because I have to explain what is going on first."

I opened the door and got out.

"Be back in a little while. We love you."

Mom had rolled her window down to talk to me.

"Okay, love you too."

I headed up to the church.

Knock, knock.

"Come in."

"Hey, Bro Gene, may I talk to you for minute?"

"Hi, Rose. Yes, come in, please, and have a seat. Is everything okay?"

"Well, yes, and no! I have a favor to ask, and I understand if you do not feel comfortable with saying 'yes.' I just want to check."

"Okay, what is it, Rose?"

"What I am about to tell you, I want to make sure you understand that I do not want anyone else to know about it until I am ready to tell them."

"You mean Garrett? I understand what you say stays between me and you."

"Okay, well, here it goes." I explained everything that had happened, and then I asked, "Would you go with us for support?"

"I would be honored to go with you guys tomorrow. I will help in any way possible. I want to reassure you, Rose, that tomorrow, keep in mind that God is always there for you, and so am I."

"Thank you, Bro Gene. We will see you tomorrow at 9:45 a.m. outside the courthouse."

"Okay, I will see you then."

As we stood up to walk out of the office, we met Garrett coming into the church.

"Hey, is everything okay? What are you doing here?" Garrett asked.

"Everything is fine. I just needed to talk to your dad for a minute. I thought you were in school."

"I was. I had to stop by to get a book from my dad. I can leave if you need to be alone with him."

"No, I am finished. I was just headed outside to wait on Mom and Dad."

I smiled.

"Oh, well, then, I will wait with you, and we can talk about what you missed today, if you want to."

Garrett smiled and opened the front door of the church.

"That would be nice, thank you."

I walked out the door, and Garrett followed me.

We talked about the homework that was assigned today, and then my Mom and Dad showed up.

"Thank you, Garrett, for everything. I will see you Sunday."

I turned and headed to the car.

"Your welcome. Have a good weekend."

He waved and headed back into the church.

"Oh, did you invite Garrett tomorrow?" Dad asked as I closed the car door.

"No, he came in when I was finished talking to Bro Gene. I asked Bro Gene though, and he said he would love to, so he is going to meet us at nine forty-five in the morning."

"Oh, that sounds great," Mom exclaimed.

* * * * *

"Now that we have heard from all the experts, I would like to call Rose to the stand to speak," Judge Barry expressed an hour into the trial; I walked slowly to the stand.

This was the first time that I had seen my biological parents in ten years, and now they were sitting there, staring at me, and on the other side of the room, my mom and dad sat looking at me. They were so worried about what could happen that Bro Gene was there for moral support.

"Rose, I would like you to tell the court how you feel about everything that is happening."

I told the court what we had talked about yesterday in the judge's chamber.

"Is there anything that you would like to say directly to your biological parents?" the judge asked me when I was finished.

"I would like to say to you that I love you the best I know how and that I forgive you for what you did, and I would like you to show me how much you love and care for me by letting me stay with the family who has taken me in and finally given me a real home and a real future."

"Thank you, Rose you may step—"

"I would like to ask Rose a few questions, if that is okay?" the attorney for my biological parents interrupted the judge.

"Oh, okay, just keep it short and to the point."

The judge smiled at me in reassurance.

"Rose, when you lived with your parents, did they do anything to physically hurt you?" he asked as he walked closer to me.

"Besides leaving me in a car for hours and never coming back, you mean?" I asked sarcastically.

"I mean, did they ever physically hit you or violate you?"

"Objection, I do not understand how this affects what we are here for," my attorney quickly stood up and proclaimed.

"Judge, I just want to prove a point. It will not take long," the attorney replied as my parents smiled like they had already won.

"You may continue, just make it quick," the judge agreed. "Rose, please answer the question," the judge asked as he looked back at me.

"When I was six, it was two days after my birthday and I had gotten two hundred dollars from my grandfather, my parents had taken the money and went out and bought alcohol. They came home, and I had been watching TV while they were gone. They told me to go to my room, and I did for a little while. When I got hungry, I came out and asked if I could have some supper. By this time, they were trashed, and they did not want me around. They told me to go back to my room and go to sleep. I told them I was hungry, and my mother got up off the couch and yelled at me to go back to my room. I guess I was not moving fast enough because she hit the back of my head, and my father had gotten up and headed toward me. He shoved me in my room, and I hit my face on the frame of the bed. That was where I got the scar right here on my forehead. It was a very traumatizing situation. The next day, everything went back to normal."

I began crying because the memory was like it was happening all over again. I had blocked it out until now.

"So you are telling me that you were abused when you were six?" the attorney asked.

"Yes, I remember that day like it was yesterday," I answered as I ran my fingers over my scar.

"You understand that you are under oath, and if you are found lying you can get in serious—"

"Objection, your honor, she answered the question. Why is he badgering the witness?" my attorney cut him off.

"Sustained, do you have any more questions? If not, you are finish," the judge snapped at the attorney.

"No further questions, your honor."

He returned to his seat.

"If there are no more questions, then I would like to take a short recess to talk to Rose's biological parents in my chamber, please."

The judge smacked his gavel, and everyone stood to their feet.

"Are you okay, Rose?" Mom and Dad asked as I walked over to them after my biological parents left the room.

"Yes, I am okay," I replied.

* * * * *

"Now that you have heard Rose speak and tell you what she wants to see you do, are you willing to drop the case?" the judge asked as my biological parents sat in his chambers with their attorney.

"Why would we do that?" my biological father asked.

"Because the daughter whom you abandoned about ten years ago told you that if you loved her at all, you would let her stay where she is," the judge explained.

"We cannot do that because of the money—" my mother blurted out without meaning to.

"Would you be quiet about that, you stupid woman," my father yelled at her.

"I don't even care what you are talking about. I want to make this very clear. This is your only opportunity to make things right with your daughter. If we leave this room and you chose to go on with this trial, then she is going to know that you do not love her enough to give her what she asked for. So what is your final decision?" the judge asked as he stood up from his chair.

"We cannot just give up on this. We have to fight to the finish," my father told the judge.

"Okay, we will see you back in the courtroom in fifteen minutes."

The judge shut the door behind them and went back to his desk to get his decision ready.

As the judge came back into the courtroom, he had a sad gleam in his eyes as he looked at me, and I knew that my parents had not done what I had asked. I did not know what was going to happen now that it was in the judge's hands. I was so scared that he was going to send me back to my real parents, and I did not want that at all.

"I have made my final decision. I want you to know that this was not a hard decision to make. A young girl needs her parents now more than anything in this fragile time in her life. I understand that both sides have different reasons for being here, and I fully believe with all my heart that my decision is what is best for Rose."

I was so nervous I wanted to scream, "What is your verdict?" I sat there, watching my parents, and they looked so happy like they already knew that I was going to have to go back with them because they did not drop the case. I knew deep down that they had something big to gain from me going home; otherwise, why would they, all of a sudden, want me back? No matter what the judge's decision would be, I was blessed to had had this last month, knowing that it was possible to be loved and be a part of a real family who wanted me.

"Now before I give you my decision, I want to make a few comments. I want to let everyone know that after I make my decision, no one is to try and leave this court until I dismiss you all. I have more than one thing to rule on today. My decision is that Rose should be now and always will be with the Thomases. They have shown her what love is and that she is an important part of their family. Now the other thing I have to rule on is that as biological parents to Rose, your parental rights have been taken away. Along with taking your rights away from Rose, it takes your rights away from her grandfather's check that he left her, and before you leave this courtroom, I will have the check in my hands. Is everyone clear on this?" he asked, looking at my biological parents.

Irene and Leon were so happy with the decision for me to stay with them they missed the check part while they were hugging me and telling me how much they loved me.

"He was my father. It should be my money, not hers," my biological father shouted as he started toward the exit where he was greeted by a police officer.

"That check was left to Rose, and if I were you, I would place it in my bailiff's hand right now or you will all spend some time in jail."

The bailiff walked over, and my biological mother placed an envelope in his hand.

"Thank you, court is dismissed. Mr. and Mrs. Thomas, may I please see you and Rose in my chambers?" Judge Barry asked.

We gathered our things and headed off to his chambers. I was relieved that it was finally over. I had no idea what he wanted us to meet with him for.

"It has come to my attention that your biological grandfather past away last week, and in his will, he left you some money," the judge explained as he handed me an envelope.

"My grandpa died. Do you know how?" I asked, trying not to cry.

My grandpa and I were close when I was little, and then when I got put into foster care, I kept in touch for a few years, and then I lost touch with him.

"No, I would not have known anything if your biological mother had not said something about money in my chambers during the trial. So I did some checking into it and found out what money they were talking about. It is yours to do as you wish with it. However, I believe that you should sit down with your new parents and discuss it when you are ready."

"Thank you, Judge Barry, for everything," I said as I stood up and headed to the door.

"Thank you, judge, we greatly appreciate everything you have done for us," Leon said as they shook hands, and we headed toward the front door of the courthouse.

"Hey, guys, I thought I would wait for you because I wanted to make sure you were still up for babysitting tonight, Rose? Because I totally understand if you do not want to come over," Gene asked as he met us outside by our cars.

"Oh, no, I am fine with coming over. It might keep my mind off things."

I smiled and placed the envelope the judge had given me in my back pocket.

"Okay, do I need to have Garrett come get you?" he replied.

"No, we will get her there, but thank you for the offer," Irene replied.

"Okay, well, then, we will see you in a few hours."

Gene gave me a hug and headed to his car.

"Okay, I will see you guys tonight," I agreed as we headed toward our car.

We got in the car and headed to get something to eat. We had been in court for hours, and we were all hungry.

"So, sweetie, do you want to talk about anything that happened today?" Irene asked as we waited for our food.

"If it is okay with you, I would like to just think about all of it before we talk."

I was not ready to talk about it, and I was not ready to look at what was in that envelope.

"That is fine, hunny. Just remember that we are here to talk when you are ready," Leon said as he delivered our food.

"I will talk soon. I promise."

"Okay, that is all we can ask."

After dinner, we headed home. It had been a long day, and all I wanted to do was get ready to go over to Bro Gene's to babysit. I had not thought about babysitting since I agreed to it almost a week ago. I hadn't even thought about Garrett going over to the cheerleader's house who really liked him.

"Hey, Rose, we want you to understand how much we love you and how much you mean to us. We do not believe in just giving you something without responsibilities, so what we are about to give you comes with responsibilities," Leon explained a few miles away from our house.

"I understand," I said, curious of what he was talking about.

"Okay, well, close your eyes and keep them closed until I tell you to open them," Irene explained as we turned on to our street.

"Okay, easy does it, just step down and then stand up, and I will lead you the rest of the way to your surprise."

Leon took my hand and led me out of the car.

"Okay, Rose, open your eyes. Surprise!" Irene yelled as I opened my eyes to find a red Mustang sitting in our driveway.

"Who's car is this?" I asked, not believing that someone bought me a car.

"This car belongs to you. However, there are rules. You have to help pay for the insurance and the gas. The car is a 'welcome to our family' gift because we were so convinced that the judge would say you could stay with us that we wanted it to be here when we got home. Do you like it?" Leon explained with a huge smile.

"I...I...I love it. I don't know what to say. I will get a job or babysit or do whatever it takes to help pay for it. Is there any way I could drive it tonight?" I asked, happier than I had ever been before.

This was the first gift anyone had ever gotten me that was not to benefit themselves like a pack of cigarettes or beer.

"Yes, we have put insurance on it and tagged it, so it is fully ready to drive. This is why we wanted to take you last week to get your license. Go get ready, and then you can drive it to Garrett's," Dad explained as they both gave me a big hug.

"Thank you both so much. I cannot believe you did this for me."

I hugged them and ran up to my room to get ready.

As I was in my room, I was thinking about all that had happened today: the huge drama in court, the getting to stay with my parents, the envelope that the judge had given me before we left, and my new car that my parents gave me. This was the best day of my life so far.

I took a shower, trying to relax from the day, and then I decided to do a little bit of homework that Garrett had told me I missed yesterday, and when it was time to go, I grabbed my purse and headed downstairs. I gave Mom and Dad a kiss and hurried out to my new car. I got in and sat there for a minute just enjoying the feeling of being in my own car. When I put my purse in the passenger seat, the letter from court fell out. I looked at it for a minute and then quickly shoved it back in my purse. I put it there when I took off my pants so that I would not see it. I did not have the courage to open it yet. I started the car and headed to Garrett's house.

Knock, knock.

"Come in," I heard from the other side of the door, so I opened the door.

"Hi, Rose, how are you today?" Melinda asked, not knowing about anything that went on today.

"I'm good. How are you?" I asked, trying to keep a smile on my face.

"I'm good. I am so glad you came to babysit. She is eating a bottle right now and will probably go to sleep in about an hour," she explained as she put on her lipstick.

"Okay, that sounds great," I said, thankful that I would be alone and just be able to think.

"Oh, hi, Rose, what are you doing here?" Garrett asked, shocked, as he entered the living room.

"I am babysitting Kylee tonight while you guys go to dinner. I hope you have a good evening."

I gave him a smile as I put my purse on the couch.

"Oh, that is great. I did not know you were the sitter," he explained.

"Honey, have you seen my keys? I cannot seem to find them anywhere?" Gene came in the living room, asking.

"Yes, dear, they are in here," Melinda answered sarcastically.

"Oh, hi, Rose, how are you doing?" Gene asked when he saw me standing there.

"I am great, thank you for asking," I replied as he gave me a hug.

"Well, we need to be going?" Melinda announced as she gave me a warm smile and headed for the door.

"Good night, guys, have fun and be careful," I said as they walked out the door.

* * * * *

"Hey, Dad, I think I am going to head home, if that is okay with you and Mom?"

"Is there any reason you want to head home?" Gene asked with a smirky smile.

"Maybe, is it okay?"

"Yes, that is fine. Do you want me to run you over there?"

"No, it is okay. I will walk. It is only a few blocks. Thank you. I will see you when you guys get home."

"Hey, son, she has had a really rough day, so if she doesn't want to talk or if she is not herself, respect her wishes and do not push," Gene explained as he walked Garrett to the front door.

"Okay, Dad, I understand," Garrett agreed.

Garrett walked the two blocks back to his house, and when he arrived, I heard him open the front door. Kylee had been asleep for about an hour, and I had been sitting on the couch, staring at the envelope from court. I tried to wipe my face so he would not know that I had been crying, but it did not seem to work.

"Are you okay, Rose?" he asked as he saw my tear-stained face and quickly sat down beside me.

"Yes, I am fine," I said as the tears started coming again.

"I am here if you need to talk," he assured me and wrapped his arm around me.

We sat there in silence for about thirty minutes before I decided I wanted him to know what happened.

"I want to talk, but I want to know first that what I tell you will not affect how you treat me, and I do not want anyone else to know."

I wanted to make sure he understood that before I told him.

"I promise I won't tell anyone, and I could never treat you differently," he assured me.

"Okay, well, here it goes…"

I told him everything that had happened up to this point. I could not believe how easy it was to talk to him. He showed no judgment and no disgust in anything I was telling him. I could talk to him all night, but my story was over. I ended at when I was staring at the envelope right before he walked in, trying to decide if I wanted to open it.

"I will sit here with you if you want me to so you can open it," he said as he brushed my hair out of my face and smiled.

"I would like that very much," I said as I picked up the envelope.

We both sat there in silence as I opened the envelope to find a check and a letter written by my grandfather before he passed away. I read the letter out loud so he could hear it and I was not alone.

My precious granddaughter Rose,

I am so sorry that I did not fight harder to keep in touch with you. The truth is I got very sick a few months after we last talked. Do you remember the last time we talked?

It was late October, and we sat on our favorite bench, down by the stream. You told me how sad you were, and I assured you that you would not always be that sad. I pray that you are not still sad. I hope that you have a family who loves you and who has shown you that what happened to you was not because of anything you did. I hope that you are happy and maybe you have even found a special boy who makes you feel like you are the queen of the world like your grandmother made me feel. When you find him, hang on to him forever.

I hope that this letter gets to you along with the money that I left for you. I want you to take this money and change the world, starting with yourself. I want you to be happy, and I want you to always remember that no matter what happens, I will love and always have loved you. I pray that God will find his way into your heart as he has mine and that I will see you in heaven someday. Keep your head up high and toward the sky. I love you so much! I hope you can forgive me for letting you go.

With all my love,
Grandpa Joe

When I finished reading the letter, my eyes were filled with tears. I had forgotten all about Garrett sitting beside me until I felt his arm around me, and he let me lay on his shoulder and cry. After a little while, I was able to get myself together and look at the check that my grandfather had given to me. I could not believe what I saw, so I had to make sure I was right.

"Does that say what I think it says, Garrett?"

"Um, well, if you think it says three million dollars, then, yes, it is what you think it is," he replied with a smile.

"Wow, I cannot believe that he gave me everything he had. No wonder they wanted me back," I said as I began to get upset because of the reason they tried to ruin my life again.

"It doesn't matter now, babe. They have no rights to come after you," Garrett reassured me.

As I was sitting there, trying to get a grip on what I had in my hand, it dawned on me that Garrett had just called me "babe." Did that mean what I think it meant or was it just an accident? I did not want to know tonight. I just wanted to enjoy lying in his arms. I was happy that I had someone to share this secret with who was my own age and could maybe understand.

* * * * *

As I woke up the next morning, I was not sure if I was truly awake because I was not in my own bedroom, and I was lying in the arms of Garrett. I could not remember anything after I read the letter and Garrett hugged me. Did his parents not come home? Did they know we were sleeping on the couch? I decided I did not want to worry about it; at that moment, all I wanted to do was enjoy the time lying with him.

"Good morning, you two, it is time to get up," Melinda said as she walked into the living room a few minutes later.

"I am so sorry. I did not mean to fall asleep. I will get out of your way," I said as I quickly sat up.

"You are just fine, sweetie. You do not have to go anywhere. You were asleep when we got home, and we called your mom and dad and told them you were asleep, and they agreed you could spend the night. I told them I would send you home after breakfast. We are getting ready to eat breakfast, and then you can do what you want."

She smiled, reassuring me everything was fine.

"Good morning, how did you sleep?" Garrett asked as he sat up behind me on the couch.

"I slept good for the first time all week. How about you?" I asked, still wondering what he meant when he called me "babe" last night.

"I slept okay. How are you feeling? Any better?" he asked as he put his hand on my shoulder.

"I feel like I am ready to put this whole thing behind me. I also feel like I am going to have to talk to my mom and dad about the check. I am not sure what they are going to think about that," I explained, hesitant.

"I will go with you if you would like moral support," he offered.

"You do not have to do that."

"I know I don't have to. However, I would like to do that for you."

"Okay, well, maybe after breakfast and after you get ready."

"Okay, then, that is what we will do."

"Breakfast is ready," we heard from the kitchen, so we headed to the table.

"Good morning, Rose, how is everything this morning?" Gene asked as he greeted me at the table.

"Everything is a lot better. Garrett and I talked about everything, and if you do not mind, you can fill in Melinda so she knows too. However, you are the only family I would like to have known if you do not mind. I am glad you guys will know, and then I want to leave it at that," I explained to both of them.

"Whatever it is, I promise I will not repeat a word," Melinda said as she dished up breakfast.

We had biscuits and gravy, eggs, and bacon.

"Thank you, that means a lot to me, Melinda."

After breakfast, I went home to get cleaned up, and Garrett was coming over to help me tell my mom and dad about the check.

After we told them about it, they seemed to be just fine with it. They told me we would go to the bank, and I could set up a checking and a savings account. I could use the money however I wanted to as long as I ran past the big stuff with them first. I could not believe that they were so understanding about it.

So that afternoon, we took the check to the bank, and Garrett stayed with me all day. I do not know what we were, but I knew I was happy being close to him.

Tomorrow was Thanksgiving, and the house was crazy busy. Mom and Dad were getting everything ready for the big dinner we were having at the church that they had every year. The church did a dinner and invited the people who had no place to go for Thanksgiving to come ate a hot home-cooked meal. It had been a few weeks since all of the court stuff, and we had all put it behind us for the most part. Garrett and I were closer than ever. However, I still did not know what we meant to each other, and for now, I was okay with that. This was the first Thanksgiving I really had something to be thankful for.

"Rose, are you ready to go to the church?" Dad asked me as I sat in my room, thinking of all the things I had to be thankful for this year.

"Yes, I will be right down," I yelled as I put a light jacket on and headed downstairs.

"Will you carry this to the car, please?" Mom asked as she handed me a basket of food.

"Sure, I will meet you at the car."

"Okay, be right there, just have to grab the last box."

Mom turned and grabbed the box on the counter, and we headed to the church.

"Is Garrett going to help us set up tables?" Dad asked as we pulled into the church parking lot.

"Yes, he is meeting us here," I replied.

"Great," Dad exclaimed.

As we walked up to the church, I saw Garrett and Rachael talking at the side of the church. I continued to help Mom and Dad carry all the boxes in before I headed over to where they were standing.

As I turned the corner, all I saw was them kissing, and my heart hit the floor, and all I thought was to get away quickly. Garrett and I had never talked about being more than friends. I just thought we were headed in that direction. I guess I was wrong. I could not believe he would try and hide something like this from me. I was so hurt, but I had to stay and help set up, so I just avoided him the whole day.

I made myself useful in any area he and Rachael were not.

After we finished working, Mom and Dad were visiting, and I decided to just walk home. I did not want to have to deal with Garrett and Rachael. As I started walking away from the church, I saw Garrett get in his truck; and shortly after, Rachael was jumping in with him. I knew I had no right to be mad because we were not boyfriend/girlfriend, but I was just sad.

When I made it home, I decided to help Mom by cleaning up the kitchen from where she had cooked all day. Then I decided to go sit in the hot tub and relax for a while before Mom and Dad got home. They made it home a few hours later.

"Hey, Rose. Garrett was asking about you after you left. He said he tried to find you all day, and you were never around. Is something going on with you two?" Dad asked as he walked out to the patio where the hot tub was.

"No, I was just busy today. I guess we just kept missing each other."

I tried to not let him read the expression on my face.

"Oh, okay, if you want to talk, we are here. Maybe you can sit with him tomorrow at dinner."

Dad tried to get me to talk; I just did not feel like talking

"Yeah, maybe, we will see."

I was sad because I was excited about spending this Thanksgiving with people I cared so much about, and now I had to avoid one of them all day.

"Dinner is almost ready, so hurry and change," Mom called as I was getting out of the hot tub.

I ran upstairs through the outside door so I would not track water in the house and quickly threw on some sweatpants and a shirt. I went downstairs and sat down for dinner. We ate in silence for the most part because we were all so tired from all the work today.

"Sweetie, we are leaving about eight o'clock in the morning. Are you going with us or are you going to meet us later? Dinner does not start until eleven," Mom asked as we cleaned off the table.

"I will meet you there before eleven o'clock, if that is okay?"

"Yes, that is fine. Just make sure you are there to help serve so we can make sure we have enough servers, okay? We are short this year, so Rachael and Garrett volunteered also. Rachael said she would take Sarah's spot since she is out of town," Mom explained.

"Oh, okay, I will make sure I am there on time."

"Good night, sweetie, we will see you in the morning."

Dad gave me a kiss on the forehead and headed off to his room.

"Good night, Mom and Dad. See you in the morning."

I went up to my room and decided to call Sarah. She had to go to her grandparent's house for the holiday because her grandmother was not doing well, and they wanted to see her in case she would not make it until Christmas.

"Hello?"

"Hey, Sarah."

"Hey, Rose! How are you doing?"

"Well, I am okay. How is your grandma?"

"She is okay. She knows who we are, and she does not look very sick."

"I am glad to hear she is doing okay while you are there."

"So what is up? Is something wrong?"

"You know me to well, Sarah."

I laughed, and then I explained everything that went on at the church.

"Are you sure he was kissing her?"

"Well it was hard to miss."

"I just don't know, Rose, because he said he could never like Rachael. She is too full of herself, and she is a very mean person. He does not like her the same way he likes you."

"Wait, what? He likes me?"

"I was not supposed to say anything, but I think it may help. Maybe you should talk to him and make sure what you saw was not a misunderstanding."

"That is kind of hard to be a misunderstanding, don't you think?"

"Talk to him. You owe him that much."

"Okay, thank you, Sarah. See you next week."

"Your welcome. Talk to you later."

We hung up the phone, and I wondered if maybe she was right. *Could what I saw be a misunderstanding? Well, then, I remember she got in the truck with him. How can I misunderstand them kissing and then her leaving with him? I didn't know what to do. Maybe I would just ask him tomorrow, and he can explain, and I can just move on.*

"Okay, sweetie, we are leaving. We will meet you at the church in a little while."

Mom smiled and grabbed her stuff.

"Okay, see you there."

I waved as I sat in front of the TV.

I had decided that I would talk to Garrett before we started serving, so I was going to drive over to his house before I went to church. I left the house about thirty minutes before I needed to be at the church, and it took me about five minutes to get to Garrett's house.

As I pulled up to his house, I noticed another car in the driveway, so I decided not to stop. I kept driving, and as I pulled away, I saw Rachael walking out of the front door. I decided I did not need to talk to him; this spoke for itself, so I went on to church.

"Hey, Mom, where do you need me to help?" I asked as I walked into the fellowship hall.

"Oh, hey, you are early, so will you go to the kitchen and please help them get everything ready?"

"Sure, Mom."

I walked into the kitchen and began putting food in the containers so they were ready to serve. When the time came to serve, someone asked me if I could stay in the kitchen and help them continue refilling the containers so they could keep up with all the people, and I was happy to help and relieved because I did not want to be on the serving line with Rachael and Garrett.

I stayed in the kitchen the whole time until it was my time to eat, and then I decided to eat in the kitchen with the other people who had no family. My parents were still working, so I did not have anyone to sit with anyways.

"Hey, Rose, are you avoiding me or something?" Garrett asked as I was walking to my car when the dinner was over.

"I am just headed home, Garrett. I will talk to you later," I said as I shut the door and drove off.

I knew that I was rude, but I did not want to have to talk to him about Rachael. When I got home, I decided to go to my room and watch a movie because my mom and dad were still at the church with the other church members.

I decided that I wanted popcorn with my movie, so while the popcorn popped, I put my PJs on and got the movie ready. I grabbed the popcorn and a soda and sat on my bed to start the movie when I heard a knock at my upstairs' outside door. I went to the door, and Garrett was standing there, knocking. I did not want to answer it, but I could not just let him stand there.

"Hey, Garrett," I greeted him as I motioned him to come in.

"Don't 'hey' me, Rose. Explain why you have been avoiding me for the past two days," he blurted out as he entered my room.

"What are you talking about?" I asked even though I already knew exactly what he was talking about.

"You know good and well what I am talking about. I don't know why, but I know you have been avoiding me. I said I would help set up for the dinner because you were going to be there, and I said I would help with the serving line because I would be with you, and then you disappear on me."

"You sure you didn't agree to help because of Rachael?" I asked sarcastically.

"What? Rachael?" There was a long silence. "What are you talking about, Rose?"

"I saw you and Rachael outside of the church kissing, and then I saw her leave with you. I was going to talk to you about it this morning, but Rachael was at your house. I was hurt. I know we are not together, but I thought you would at least tell your best friend that you are seeing Rachael. I did not want to be around you guys because it hurt too bad. I am sorry for how I treated you. I am happy for you and for Rachael. I hope we can still be friends," I explained.

"What!" Garrett exclaimed surprisingly. "I think you read everything the wrong way."

"How can I read a kiss the wrong way and her in your truck leaving with you shortly after?" I asked as we sat on the bed.

"She kissed me, and I pulled her off and told her to stop. Then when I was leaving, she jumped in my truck without being invited and wanted to talk, so I gave her a ride home. I explained to her on the ride home that I did not like her in that way and that I liked someone else. I told her that she had to stop obsessing over me and leave me alone. Then when you saw her at my house, she came over to tell me she was sorry for everything and that she would leave me alone. I am sorry this ruined your Thanksgiving. I know you were looking forward to this Thanksgiving," he explained.

"I am so sorry that I jumped to conclusions. I had no right to even make a scene about it," I apologized.

"It is okay. I am kinda glad you got upset because that lets me know you like me," he joked.

"What! I did not say that I just—"

He brushed my hair back away from my face and kissed me in the middle of my sentence. His touch was a gentle, warm touch that melted my heart. I had never kissed a boy before, and it was the perfect moment for me. When he stopped kissing me, I did not know what to say. My brain had shut down, and I just sat there in shock.

"Now you were saying?"

He laughed.

"What does this mean?" I asked, finally getting my speech back.

"It means, Rose, would you be my girlfriend?" he asked as he took my hand.

"I would love to, Garrett," I replied as I gave him another kiss. "Do you want to watch a movie with me?" I asked as I got him a soda.

"Sure, I would love to," he replied as he got comfortable on my bed.

We were lying on the bed, watching the movie, when my parents got home. They came in to let me know they were home. They never cared when Garrett was in my room as long as we kept the door open, even when we were just friends.

"Thank you both for all your help today."

Dad smiled as he walked out of the room.

"You're welcome," we both replied together.

When the movie was over, Garrett stood up and headed toward the door.

"Hey, Rose, would you like to go out on a date with me Saturday?"

"I would love to go out with you on Saturday," I replied as I walked over to the door.

He gave me a kiss good night, and he left.

Saturday morning, I told Mom and Dad that I was going out with Garrett, and they were both excited for me. If you had asked me a year ago if I could ever picture myself happy, I would have never believed it. While I was marveling in my wonderful life, I felt a gut feeling that something was wrong. It felt like something was tugging at me. I did not want anything to ruin my date, so I just ignored the tugging.

The doorbell rang promptly at five o'clock.

"Hello, Garrett," my dad greeted him as he let him in the door.

"Hello, Mr. Thomas."

I had never actually heard Garrett call my dad "Mr. Thomas" before.

"Please call me Leon," Dad insisted.

"Okay, Leon, is Rose ready to go?" he replied.

"She should be down quickly. Where are you two going tonight?"

"I am taking her out to dinner, and then I have tickets to a concert at our church, if that is okay?"

"That is fine with me. Who are you seeing?"

"It is a band called Casting Crowns. They are a Christian group, and I am hoping that it touches Rose."

"That is a sweet gesture. After everything Rose has been through, I think the one thing she needs is salvation. We have talked to her about it, but she is not very receptive to talking about it. So I pray that you have a better time at it than we do," Dad said as he placed his hand on Garrett's shoulder.

"I hope so also. God changed my life when I accepted him as Lord and Savior of my life. I want to share that blessing with everyone, and I feel that over her lifetime, not too many people have tried to share the Word of God with Rose."

Garrett stopped talking as he looked up to see me walking into the room. I was wearing a dress that stopped at my knees and was a baby blue color. I had a white sweater over it. I was wearing light-blue shoes that had a very low heel on them. Irene had helped me curl my hair and pin some of it out of my face.

"Wow, you look amazing," Garrett expressed as he greeted me.

"Thank you," I replied.

"Well, you two better get going. You don't want to be late," Dad said as he gave me a kiss and opened the front door.

"Good night, Mom and Dad."

I gave Mom a kiss, and we headed out of the house.

We pulled up to a beautiful restaurant where Garrett got out and walked over to open my door. We went in and got seated right away. We had a fabulous dinner, and then he told me we were going to a concert. The only concert I had ever been to was a school concert where I had to babysit my foster parent's kids. The concert was packed. We found a seat not too far from the front.

"Would you like a drink or anything?" Garrett asked as we sat down.

"Yes, please," I replied as he headed to the lobby where they were selling refreshments.

While Garrett was gone, I watched the pictures on the big screens that they had hanging from the ceiling. As I was watching, a saying came up that said, "Fear not, for I am with you; Be not dismayed, for I am your God. I will strengthen you, Yes, I will help you, I will uphold you with My righteous right hand" (Isaiah 41:10). I used to go to church as a child, and everyone always said that God would always be with you and never forsake you. My biological parents were always mean to me, and then when they left me, I was so mad at God because he let this happen, and the more I moved, the more I got mad at God. I thought if I started going to church with Mom and Dad, it would help me got over being mad, but it had not helped.

"Here is your drink, Rose," Garrett said.

"Oh, thank you."

"Is everything okay? It looked like I startled you?"

"Yes, everything is fine. I was just in a daze, I guess."

I smiled, trying to convince him that everything was really okay.

"All right, I think they are about to start."

He sat beside me and put his arm around me.

All I could think about the whole night was the Scripture I had seen before they started playing. While they were in the middle of a slow song, I felt that tugging again that I had felt at the house. I tried to ignore it, but it would not go away. The song finally ended, and so did the concert.

"Did you like the concert?" Garrett asked as we walked to the car.

"I did. It was a great concert."

"Well, can I ask you a question?"

"Sure," I answered, not sure where this was going.

As Garrett got in the car, he asked, "If you were to die today, do you know if you would go to heaven or hell?"

"Um, well, the way my life has been, probably hell," I replied.

"May I share something with you?"

"Sure."

I still wasn't sure where he was going.

"John 3:16 says, 'For God so loved the world that he gave his only begotten son, that whosoever believeth in him should not perish, but have everlasting life.' Do you know God as your personal savior, Rose?"

"No."

"I want to share my testimony with you, if that is okay?"

"What is a testimony?"

"It is how God changed my life."

"Okay, go ahead."

"I was saved a few years ago. I have grown up in church my whole life because my father was a preacher. All through school, everyone always thought that I knew everything about the Bible because of my dad. They always made fun of me for being a preacher's kid or a PK.

It made me so mad. I was mad at my dad for being a preacher, and I was mad at God for allowing me to go through the torture.

"One day, I heard a preacher say God would never give you more than you could handle. God would never leave you. He would always be with you through it all. I thought about that for a while, and I knew that being a PK was not the problem, neither was being made fun of. Everyone was made fun of at one point or another. The problem was I was not living the way God wanted me to. I would disrespect my parents and teachers, and I would curse the people who were teasing me.

"I came to realize that I needed God in my life. I accepted him as my Savior and asked him to come into my heart. I was able to forgive the kids who were teasing me and was able to stop acting the way I was. After accepting Christ as my Savior, I stopped cursing and was able to start respecting my parents and my teachers. God helped me grow and learn from his word, and I live every day according to the Word of God."

"That is a very touching story, but I have so much hate in me, Garrett, that God doesn't want me," I told him.

"God wants everyone who is willing to ask him to come into their hearts and live for him," he responded.

"I just don't know, Garrett."

As we were talking, I got that tugging feeling again.

"Okay, well, think about it, and we can talk more another time," Garrett assured me.

"Let's go home, Garrett."

I did not want to talk about this anymore.

As we pulled into my driveway, Garrett turned the car off and got out to walk me to my door. It was late, so we went to my bedroom door so I would not wake my parents.

"Good night, Rose. I hope you think about what we talked about."

"Good night, Garrett. I will see you tomorrow at church."

"Okay, I will see you there."

Garrett touched the side of my face with his soft hand and gave me a good-night kiss.

I lay awake most of the night thinking about what Garrett had talked to me about on our date. *Could God really care that much about me? Could he really want me to trust him with my heart and ask him to come live in me?* Everything was so confusing, and I did not know how I could ever forgive God for what he had done to me. I quickly got up and got ready for church before I headed down to breakfast.

"So, sweetie, how was your date last night?" Mom asked as I sat down at the table.

"Dinner was fabulous, and so was the concert. I had a great time, thank you for letting me go," I replied as I began to eat the pancakes that Mom had made for me.

"I am so glad to hear that. So you really like Garrett, don't you?" Dad asked as he sat down at the table.

"Yes, I do. That really scares me though because I have never felt this way about a guy before."

"It is okay to feel this way about a guy. Just think that God sent you to us, and maybe he sent Garrett to you so that you could finally be happy," Dad explained.

"I just feel that if I get to close to him, then he will leave because everyone I have gotten close to in the past has left me," I explained.

"Just remember that God will never give you anything that you cannot handle," Mom explained as she handed me the plate of pancakes.

"I am just scared. My whole life has changed since I have been living here, and I am just trying to let go of the past."

I placed the plate of pancakes next to my father when I stopped talking.

"Do you know that no matter what you have gone through, God is always there for you, and he loves you, and he wants you to turn to him for comfort. In Psalm 91: 4–5, it says, 'He shall cover you with his feathers, and under his wings you shall take refuge; His truth shall be your shield and buckler. You shall not be afraid.' Trust him, and he will give you strength."

Dad smiled and placed his hand on mine.

"That is what Garrett talked to me about last night after the concert. Do you really think that God wants me to let him come live in my heart? Do you think that he can forgive me for the hatred I have carried toward him all these years?"

"In Acts 3:19, it says, 'Repent therefore and be converted, that your sins may be blotted out, so that times of refreshing may come from the presence of the Lord.' Trust the Lord as your Savior and ask him to come live in your heart, and he will forgive you and live in you," Dad explained.

"I am going to go grab my jacket for church."

I changed the subject as I got up and headed upstairs.

When I came back down, the table was all cleaned off, and my parents were grabbing their coats. I was hoping that they would not bring the breakfast topic back up on the way to church.

"So, Rose, do you think that Garrett would like to come over for dinner one night this week?" Mom asked as we headed to church.

"I don't know, but I bet he would love to. I will ask him after church," I replied, relieved that she had started a different conversation.

As we got to the church, I saw Garrett standing outside, talking to some friends. As we parked and got out, I smiled at my parents and then headed over to meet Garrett. I usually sat with Garrett and the other youth during services. We went to Sunday school, and just like a brick being shoved into my stomach, our youth pastor brought back up the topic my dad was covering at breakfast.

"Okay, I want you all to calm down and listen. Today, I want to talk to you all about becoming a Christian. Most of you have been coming to church most of your life, and some of you have only been going to church a little while. Going to church for your whole life does not make you a Christian. Doing good deeds all the time is not going to get you into heaven. There are three steps you need to do to become a Christian," the youth pastor explained.

As I sat there in my seat next to Garrett, I started thinking about the last three conversations I had. They all were about the same thing: becoming a Christian. Every time the subject came up, I felt like there was something in the pit of my stomach. I decided right there in the youth classroom that maybe God was trying to tell me something. So I decided to listen and not just shrug the topic off.

"These three steps are as easy as your ABCs," the youth pastor interrupted my thoughts. "The first step is A: to admit that you are a sinner. You have to admit to God that you are a sinner. Then there is B: believe that Jesus is the son of God. You have to believe that Jesus died on the cross and rose from the grave and that he is coming back. The final step is C: confess your faith in Jesus. Ask Jesus to come into your heart and forgive you of your sins. Then share your faith with other people."

He paused for a minute, and the whole room was silent.

Is it that simple? I finally understood what it meant to become a Christian.

As the youth pastor kept talking, I felt that this was what God was trying to tell me. I thought back on my life and began to look at it in a different view. If my parents had not left me on that night, then I would not have been moved around so much, and I would not have been placed with this amazing family. I believe that everything that happened to me in the past had led me to this moment, and that was God's purpose in my life.

"Are you one of the people who need to pray and accept Jesus as your Lord and Savior?" the youth pastor asked, interrupting my thoughts again.

"I would like everyone to bow their heads and close their eyes. If you want to accept Jesus as your Lord and Savior and you believe that he is the son of God, then say this prayer with me. 'Lord, I know that I am a sinner. I know that I have been living my own way, and I want to change. Lord, I believe that you died on that cross for my sins and that you rose from the grave. I believe that you are coming back again. Lord, please come into my heart and save me. I lay everything at the cross, and I will follow you.' If you said this prayer, I want you to raise your hand. Every head is still bowed, and every eye is closed."

He paused for a few minutes, then continued.

"Now to those of you who raised your hand or who prayed this prayer and did not raise your hand, will you take that next step and stay after I dismiss the class? I want to talk to you for a minute and pray with you. Thank you, class, for being here today. Let's go to the Lord in prayer. Garrett, will you, please, close us in prayer?"

After Garrett prayed, everyone left the room. Garrett did not even motion for me to go with him; it was like he already knew that I had accepted Christ during class.

I was the only one left in the room when the youth pastor approached me. We talked for a while, and he asked me if I would go forward in church and let the congregation know that I had made this decision so that they could pray for me, and he explained to me about being baptized and that it was a symbolization to show the people that I had been dead of the world and resurrected with Christ.

When he was finished talking, we slipped into the back of the church where the youth group was sitting. When I sat down beside Garrett, he took my hand and gave me a warm smile. The feeling I had in the pit of my stomach had finally gone away, and as the pastor talked, I finally understood and really listened to what he was saying.

After church, I walked down the aisle with my youth pastor and told the church that I had accepted Jesus as my Lord and Savior and that I wanted to follow in baptism. After the final prayer, I stood at the back of the church for my fellow brothers and sisters in Christ to welcome me into the family of Christ.

"We love you so much, Rose, and we are so proud that you have made this decision."

Mom and Dad waited to be the last in line so that they could walk out with me. This was the best moment of my entire life.

Almost a month had passed since I invited Christ into my heart. My life had changed in so many ways since that day at church. I did not harbor hatred in my heart anymore. I felt like a huge weight had been lifted off my shoulders. I found myself listening to Christian music artists to inspire me instead of the rap music I used to listen to. Garrett and I had been together almost every night for the past month. It was almost Christmas, and I could not wait to spend our first Christmas together. Garrett and his family had to leave town for the first week of Christmas break, and I had been going insane without him. He would return home in just two short days, so Mom and I were going Christmas shopping to find the perfect gift for him.

"So, Rose, are you excited that Garrett is coming home in a few days?" Mom asked as we headed to the mall.

"I am so excited. I cannot believe he has only been gone for five days," I replied.

"So who is left on our shopping list for today?" Mom asked, smiling.

"Well, let's see. We have Dad, our secret sisters at church, Garrett, and then we have the children we are sponsoring at the hospital," I read off the list.

Dad decided he did not want to shop today, so he stayed home.

"What are you going to get Garrett?" Mom asked as we parked the car and headed to the front door.

"I'm not sure yet. I know that he said he needs a new Bible because the one he has got water dumped on it by his sister. I also thought I might get him some clothes. What do you think?" I asked Mom after giving her my ideas.

"I think that both of those ideas are great," Mom replied.

We shopped for hours before finally finishing all our Christmas shopping. We ended the day by taking a picture with Santa. This was the first year in my whole life that I knew the real reason for the season. My whole life, I had taken pictures with Santa only because I had to take the little kids and watch my foster parents got drunk after dinner. This year was going to be different. There was only twelve days until Christmas, and I was excited because I had been invited to spend Christmas Eve with Garrett and his family. Christmas was on a Friday this year, so Mom and Dad decided that we would wait until Saturday to go see their families so that I could spend time with Garrett's family and Garrett could spend Christmas morning with me and my family.

"Okay, so we got everything on our list, and we are finished for the most part," Mom commented.

"Yes, I have a few more gifts I want to buy, but I am going to get them with Garrett when he gets back," I confirmed.

"That is great!"

Mom smiled as we headed home.

When we got home, Dad was cooking supper for us. We were shocked that he had already set the table and was ready to eat when we finished bringing in the presents. I brought the presents that we did not want Dad to see to my room through the outside door.

"So did you guys have fun shopping today?" Dad asked as he sat the last dish on the table.

"We had a lot of fun, and we finished all our shopping except for a few little items," Mom filled him in.

"Great, does that mean that you spent all of my money?" Dad joked.

"Not all of it, just most of it," I chuckled.

We sat in silence, eating the wonderful dinner Dad had cooked.

"Oh, Rose, I almost forgot to tell you that Garrett called while you were gone and asked if you would call him when you got home. There was something important he needed to talk to you about," Dad said as we were finishing up dinner.

"Really! May I be excused and go call him?" I asked, trying not to jump up and run.

"Yes, sweetie, go call him," Mom said with a big grin on her face.

Ring, ring.

"Hello?"

"Hi, is Garrett there?"

"Yes, one moment, please."

"This is Garrett."

"Hi, Garrett, it's Rose."

"Hi, Rose, how are you doing?"

"I'm good. How are you?"

"I'm okay."

"My dad said you needed to tell me something important."

"Yes, I know that you were expecting me home in a few days, but I will not be home in a few days."

"Aw, why not?"

"Well, don't be mad, but I am home now and would love for you to come over."

"What!" I screamed and hung up the phone.

I ran downstairs and told Mom and Dad I was going to Garrett's and that I would be back soon. They said "okay," and I was out the door and in my car before I could fully grasp what I was doing.

I pulled up to his house and jumped out of the car as soon as I turned off the ignition. Garrett must have known that I would be over as soon as he said that because he was sitting outside on the patio.

"You're really here!" I yelled as I ran to the patio.

"I thought that might get you here pretty fast."

Garrett smiled as he grabbed me and kissed me.

I had missed him so much over the last few days. I just enjoyed him holding me until a young guy walked out to the patio and interrupted us.

"So is this the hottie you have been talking about for the last four days and would not shut up about?" the boy asked as he joined us.

"Um, hi, I'm Rose," I replied, holding my hand out to shake his.

"I know who you are," he said as he pushed through me and Garrett and sat between us.

I just looked at Garrett and did not know what to think.

"Dude, that was rude," Garrett said as he walked around the boy and sat beside me. "Rose, this is my cousin John. He is staying with us for a while," Garrett said as he took my hand.

"It is nice to meet you, John," I replied.

"Sure, it is," John shot back, rolling his eyes.

"Sorry about that, honey. I cannot believe that he was so rude," Garrett expressed as we went up to his room to be alone.

"That's okay," I replied.

"So what do you want to do tomorrow?" Garrett asked, changing the subject.

"I would love to go Christmas shopping with you if you are up for it. I need to get your parents something, and I want to get a few more things for your sister," I said, smiling.

"That sounds like a good idea because I need help getting your parents something."

Garrett smiled.

"Great, well, we can leave about ten o'clock in the morning, and we could grab something to eat before we start shopping, if that is okay with you?" I suggested.

"That sounds great. Would you like to pick me up? Because I can't use Mom's car, so we will have to take yours if we can," Garrett explained.

He did not have his own truck because his dad's car broke down, and he had to take Garrett's truck until his could get fixed.

"That is fine. I will pick you up by ten. I better get back home. I just kind of ran out on Mom and Dad because I was so excited," I replied.

"Okay, I will see you in the morning."

Garrett gave me a soft kiss and walked me to my car. I drove home so happy that Garrett was finally home.

* * * * *

"Good morning, Garrett."

"Good morning, beautiful."

"Blah, am I going to have to listen to that all day long?"

"I'm sorry, all day long?"

I was puzzled by John's response.

"Mom and Dad asked if John could go with us to the mall. I told them I had to talk to you first," Garrett replied.

"Oh, I see." I paused. "I guess that is okay as long as he sits in the back and minds his own business," I finally agreed.

"Okay, thanks, sweetie," Garrett said as he gave me a light kiss on the cheek and opened my door for me.

Even though we took my car, he drove. He was such a gentleman.

"So what are your plans for tomorrow, Rose? Do you go to that boring church like the rest of them?" John asked as we headed toward the mall.

"No, I go to the wonderful church your uncle preaches at," I replied with a smile.

"John has never liked church, but since he is staying with us, he is going to try and make the best of it, and who knows, he might learn something," Garrett added.

"Yeah, learn something in church, that'll be the day."

John chuckled.

* * * * *

I woke up with an overwhelming amount of joy, knowing that it was going to be my first happy Christmas. I began getting dressed to join my family in the kitchen.

"Good morning, Rose, how are you?" Irene greeted me as I entered the kitchen.

"I'm great. How are you?"

"I got up early to start baking, and I am almost done."

I looked around the kitchen and found that Mom had filled twelve baskets with goodies.

"Mom, what are you going to do with all of the baskets?" I asked as I examined one of the baskets.

"I am going to deliver them to some of the church members."

"That sounds great, Mom. Do you need any help?"

"I was hoping you would ask. I was wondering if you would be interested in delivering one to the pastor's house?" Mom said as a grin covered her face.

"I would love to," I replied, returning the smile.

I couldn't wait to see Garrett. Every time I thought about him, I got butterflies in my stomach. I was so glad God brought me to this town and this family.

I took the basket and went to my car. As I walked to my car, I thought about the present I got Garrett and my game plan for when I wanted to give it to him. We made plans to exchange gifts Christmas night when it was just the two of us.

As I pulled into Garrett's driveway, my heart skipped a beat. All of a sudden, I was very nervous and could not figure out why. I got out of my car, grabbed the basket of goodies, and headed toward the door.

"Hi, Rose," Melinda greeted me as she opened the door.

"Hi, Melinda! Mom made you guys a goody basket and asked me to deliver it."

"And I'm sure it broke your heart to have to deliver it," Melinda said sarcastically with a smile.

"It did. I was so upset," I replied sarcastically as a big smile crossed my face.

"Well, thank you, and tell your mom I said 'thank you.'"

"I will tell her."

"Garrett's in his room if you want to go up," Melinda said, letting me enter the house.

"Thanks."

I smiled and headed upstairs.

Knock, knock.

"Come in."

"Hi, Garrett," I said as I opened his door.

"Hi, Rose," he replied as he stood up from his desk and greeted me with a brisk kiss on the cheek.

"Hi, how are you?"

I smiled.

"I'm good. I didn't think I was going to see you until later," Garrett replied.

"My mom asked me to deliver a goody basket to your mom, so I wanted to come say 'hi.'"

"Hi," he snickered.

"I have to get back to the house and help Mom, but I will see you later, right?"

"Yes, of course, you will."

He took my hand and gently brushed his lips against mine.

I headed downstairs and could not stop thinking about seeing Garrett later.

This afternoon, I was having Christmas with Mom, Dad, and Garrett, then staying the night with Melinda and Gene. I was helping them set up for the church's community Christmas dinner early while Mom and Dad finish cooking the food, so I was doing Christmas with Garrett's family Christmas Eve night and just crashing on the couch.

When I arrived at home, Mom and Dad had put all the presents under the tree and filled the stockings that were hung on the fireplace.

"We know this is your first Christmas with us, so we wanted to make it special," Mom said, seeing the surprised look on my face.

"Wow, you guys went all out, didn't you?" I whispered, still amazed.

"I just have to finish lunch, and after lunch, we will open presents."

Mom gave me a kiss and headed to the kitchen.

"What time is Garrett coming over?" Dad asked as I stared at the tree.

"He should be here around eleven," I replied, breaking away from the tree.

"Great, you better go get ready. I'm sure you want to change out of that sweats outfit."

Dad gave me a sneaky grin, and I headed upstairs to get dressed.

As I placed my last shoe on, I heard the doorbell and quickly ran downstairs.

"Hi, Garrett," my dad opened the door and greeted Garrett.

"Hi, Leon, how are you?" Garrett replied.

"Good, thanks, come on in. I will take those for you."

Dad generously took the gifts Garrett brought and placed them under the tree.

"Hi, Garrett," I said as I entered the living room.

"Hi," Garrett replied as a smile stretched from ear to ear across his face.

"Okay, you two lovebirds let's eat," Dad announced, placing one arm around my shoulders and one on Garrett's shoulder's

"Dad," I chimed as I felt my cheeks turn red.

"Dinner is served."

Mom came into the dining room carrying her famous hillbilly goulash.

"I know it doesn't look great, but it is Rose's favorite," Mom assured Garrett.

After dinner, we opened presents and told stories. We laughed, we cried, and we had a great time. I could not imagine a better Christmas, and this Christmas was not over.

After we finished cleaning everything up, we said "goodbye" to my parents and headed to Garrett's house.

When we arrived at Garrett's, no one was home, so we decided to call and see where they were.

"Hi, Mom, I was just wondering where you were. Rose and I just got home."

"Hi, sweetie, we ran to the church and brought everyone with us, but we will be home soon."

"Okay, we will just wait for you. Anything we can do to get dinner ready?"

"Yes, please put the ham in the oven so it will be done. We should be home in thirty to forty-five minutes, and I can do the mashed potatoes and veggies."

"Okay, I can do that. See you when you get home. Love you."

"Love you too. Bye."

Garrett hung up, and we went into the kitchen to put the ham on. While we were talking, we decided to peel the potatoes and get them on as well.

"So, Rose, what is your favorite Christmas memory?" Garrett asked as he pulled the potatoes out of the refrigerator.

"This Christmas."

I winked.

"I mean, besides this Christmas, silly."

"Well, it would have to be the last real Christmas celebration I had. When I was five, my grandfather took me to a cabin all decorated for Christmas. It was just me and him drinking hot chocolate by the fire and reading the story of Jesus. No parents arguing or yelling at me, just me and Grandpappy. I held on to that memory and replayed it every year, no matter where I was."

"Wow," Garrett managed to say after a few seconds of silence.

"So what is your favorite Christmas memory, Garrett?"

"Well, that would be this Christmas, but before that, it was five years ago. The first year I helped with the community Christmas dinner, a man came up to me and asked me why I was serving on Christmas day, and I shared my testimony with him and led him to Christ that Christmas day. I have never forgotten the look in his eyes, and he has been going to our church ever since, and he helps with the dinner every year since that day."

I couldn't say anything. I wiped a tear from my eyes and smiled.

We finished dinner and set the table while telling more stories. When we got everything finished and on the table, it was five o'clock. While Garrett sat the last bowl of veggies on the table, Melinda and Gene walked through the door, followed by John and Keely.

"Wow, you guys did everything," Gene exclaimed as they walked into the dining room.

"We wanted to surprise you," I said, pulling Gene's chair out for him.

"Dinner is served," Garrett added, pulling Melinda's chair out for her.

"You two are show-offs," John chimed in as he pulled his own chair out.

After dinner, I helped Garrett clear the table while Melinda got Kylee into her pajamas. Gene got the presents ready, and John continued to mouth about Garrett and me being kiss-ups.

"Okay, kids, time to open presents," Gene yelled, getting everyone's attention.

"Where are my presents?" John asked rudely.

"We have a tradition in this house, John. We open one present at a time, and guests go first," Melinda explained.

"I am a guest, and I want to go first," he whined.

"If you want to be rude and not follow this rule, then you do not need any presents," Gene gave John his serious look to let John knew he was not playing around.

"Fine," John mumbled under his breath.

Each one of us opened a present and then another until all the presents were open. The evening went very similar to the afternoon with my parents. We laughed, sang, and told stories. After all the presents were opened and the mess was cleaned up, Gene made an announcement.

"It is time to gather around and read the Christmas story."

"We read the story every Christmas Eve. It is tradition," Garrett whispered to me.

As I sat there listening to the Christmas story, I thought of Grandpappy and the last Christmas I spent with him. Garrett must have known what I was thinking about because he squeezed my hand and said, "He is watching over you, and you will see him again."

I smiled and squeezed his hand back. When the story was over, everyone went to bed, and I lay on the couch, replaying everything that had happened in the last twenty-four hours. I found myself unable to sleep, so when morning came, I decided to make breakfast for everyone. Making breakfast for everyone when I wanted to was so different from when I had to because the foster parents I had at the time were passed out.

After breakfast, we all headed to the church. We had to set up tables and chairs and prepare the serving lines. People began arriving at eleven o'clock and didn't stop until about one thirty.

"Hey, Rose, are you ready? We have to get going," Garrett asked as he walked up on Sarah and me cleaning tables.

"Go? Go where? And shouldn't we help cleanup first?"

"Where is a surprise, and there are enough volunteers to spare us, so we need to get going."

A mysterious twinkle appeared in Garrett's eyes as he talked.

"Okay, give me a minute to tell Mom and Dad. I will meet you out front," I replied as he walked off.

I told Sarah "goodbye" and headed to find my parents.

"Hey, Mom and Dad, Garrett and I are going to take off, if that is okay?"

"That's great, hunny. Have fun, and we will see you later," they quickly agreed very happily, like they knew what was going on.

"Okay. See you later. Love you."

I gave them a hug and kiss and went to meet Garrett.

As we turned down a dirt road outside of town, I tried to figure out where we were going. As we came to a stop, in front of us was a cabin with nothing around us for miles.

"Garrett, what are we doing here?" I asked as I got out of the car.

"This is part of your Christmas present," he replied, taking my hand.

As we walked into the cabin, I could smell the fresh pine tree that was decorated for Christmas. The fireplace was already going, and while I was being mesmerized by all the decorations, Garrett slipped into the kitchen to make us some hot chocolate.

"Here is your hot chocolate, madam," Garrett interrupted my thoughts.

"How…I…I don't understand. I just told you about this memory last night. How did you do all of this?" I managed to say as I took the hot chocolate from him.

"I have a few connections."

Garrett laughed.

We sat and talked for hours. We exchanged gifts, and when I looked at the clock, it was two o'clock in the morning.

"Garrett, I have to get home."

"No, it's okay. Your parents know where you are. They said we could stay tonight as long as we promise to behave and no funny business."

"Okay."

I laughed, just picturing my dad telling Garrett that. This is the best ending to one amazing Christmas.

It had been seven months now since I came to live with the Thomas family. Everything had been going great. Garrett and I were closer than ever, and even our families were closer. We had started a tradition where one night a week we had game night and alternated which house we had it at. Garrett's cousin finally went home, and school was out for the summer. Mom and Dad had asked me to meet them for lunch today because they had something important to tell me. I was heading to the restaurant now.

"Hi, sweetie," Mom softly yelled across the restaurant when I walked in.

"Hi, Mom. Hi, Dad," I greeted them both with a kiss.

"We have asked you here because we want to talk to you about something very important," Mom said while we waited for our food.

"We would like to make you an official part of this family if you would let us," Leon continued.

"I thought I was a part of the family," I said, confused.

"Well, you are, but technically, you are still a child of the state, and we want to adopt you," Irene explained.

"Oh, I see. You know I turn eighteen in a few months, right?"

"Yes, and that is one reason we want to adopt you. We want to give you our last name and reassure you that even when you turn eighteen, you are still a part of this family," Leon said as he placed my hand in his.

"I would love to become a Thomas," I said enthusiastically.

"Great, we have an appointment with Judge Barry at two o'clock this afternoon."

Leon smiled.

"Great," I replied.

We went to the courthouse after we ate and made it official. As we were driving home, I realized I would always be a part of this family.

"Surprise!" Garrett, Sarah, Gene, and Melinda yelled as we walked into our house.

They were throwing me a surprise party for my adoption, and I was very surprised.

As I was hanging out with Sarah and Garrett, talking about what had happened, there was a knock at the door.

"I'll get it," I yelled as I walked to the front door.

"Hi," I said as I opened the door.

"Hi, are you Rose?"

"Yes, and you are?"

"I am Macy, your sister."

Garrett had come up behind me because when I felt my heart skipped a beat, he placed his hand on my shoulder.

"Let's step outside, please," I motioned, then turned to Garrett. "I will be right back, and please don't say anything about who it is yet."

"Okay, I won't," he agreed, gently kissing me on the cheek, reassuring me everything was going to be okay.

"Garrett, where's the party girl?" Gene asked as Garrett rejoined the group.

"She will be right back," he replied.

Outside

"What do you mean you are my sister?" I asked, still in shock.

"Well, I am your half sister. Your dad is my dad, and we have different moms."

I sat there listening as she continued her story.

"I lived with my mom until a few months ago when she passed away, and then I came to live with Dad. I met Dad about two years ago and have grown very close to him. I stayed with him last summer, and that was when I found out about you. After Mom passed away, I took the opportunity to live with Dad and get to know your mom better. I miss my mom, but I really like living with Dad."

"Okay, okay, but why are you here and what do you want?" I blurted out, knowing she wanted something from me.

"Oh, sorry, I am just going on and on," she replied.

"I am here to ask you a huge favor. I know you don't know me, but please, please think about what I'm asking."

"I figured. What could you possibly need from me?" I asked, praying it was not money, but if I had known what it was she was about to ask me, I would have prayed for it to be money.

"Can we please sit down?"

She walked over to the porch swing and took a seat.

"Okay."

I joined her and waited for her to talk.

"Well, you see, a few months ago, Dad found out some bad news, and we thought we had a solution, but it didn't work out. Dad needs a kidney transplant, and he had a donor, but something happened, and it didn't work out." She paused. "I took a test to see if I was a match, and so did your mom, and neither one of us were a match. The doctor said he has a couple of months, maybe, to live if he does not get the transplant, and family is the best chance he has," she continued.

"And what does this have to do with me?" I asked, pretty sure I knew where she was going.

"Well, Rose, because you are his biological child, you have a good chance of being a match. I know that they have never really been parents to you, but they are the only family I have. I was hoping you would consider getting tested to see if you could help him. If you don't want to do it for them, please consider doing it for me. I don't want to lose another parent."

Macy looked into my eyes with sadness reflecting in hers.

"I will think about it, but I have to talk to my parents because they have a say also."

I smiled, trying to comfort her.

"Okay, please don't take too long. He is very sick."

She stood up to leave.

"Call me next week, and I will have an answer."

I handed her a card and walked her to the steps.

"Thanks, it was nice to meet you. Sorry it was under these circumstances."

She took the card and smiled.

"You too. Talk to you next week," I replied.

Macy walked to her car and drove out of sight.

I walked back to the swing and sat down. I needed to take a deep breath before going inside.

Lord,

> Please give me strength and courage to do the right thing. I know that everything happens for a reason, and I fully put my trust in you. In Jesus's name, amen.

I sat on the swing a few seconds, then decided to rejoin the party.

"There you are, Rose."

Sarah smiled.

"Sorry, I just needed some fresh air."

I tried to smile as I joined everyone in the living room.

"We were about to send out a search party," Gene joked.

"Is everything okay?" Garrett whispered in my ear as he walked up behind me and wrapped his arms around me.

"Later," I whispered back, not wanting anyone else to know what happened.

"Okay."

He released me from his hug and grabbed my hand, and we joined Sarah on the couch.

* * * * *

"So, sweetie, do you want to talk about it?" Garrett asked, joining me on the porch swing.

Everyone else had gone home, and Mom and Dad had turned in for the night.

"I don't know. Can we just sit here for a while?"

"We can do whatever you want to do," he replied as I placed my head on his chest.

We sat there for a while before I decided to tell him what happened.

"I am telling Mom and Dad tomorrow before they go to work," I said as I finished the story.

"Do you want me to be there?" Garrett asked.

"No, I want to do it by myself, but thank you."

I smiled and snuggled back into his arms.

The next morning came quickly, and it was time to tell my parents. I was extremely nervous because this was the first thing I was telling them as their legal daughter, and it was about my sister I never knew I had.

"Mom, Dad, I need to talk to you about something that happened last night."

I pulled up a chair and joined my parents in the kitchen.

"Is this about why you disappeared for a while?" Dad asked.

"Yes, last night, when I went to answer the door, a girl was there, and her name was Macy."

I went on to explain what happened. I waited to see how they would respond.

"Wow! The Lord works in mysterious ways."

Irene finally broke the silence with a light chuckle.

"What do you mean?" I asked, confused.

"You see, Rose, God loves everyone, no matter what they do or have done. God wants us to show his love to others. Your biological parents caused you a lot of pain and suffering, but God took that pain and suffering away. After all the bad they have done to you, they have done at least one good thing, and that was they had you, and that is a wonderful blessing. We should strive to show others the love that God has shown us on a daily basis," Dad explained as he patted my hand.

"Don't get us wrong, we are not saying you have to do it. We are saying pray about it and make a decision," Irene added.

"Okay, I will think about it. Macy is going to call me next week for a decision." I smiled. "Thank you both for your advice. I will see you guys tonight."

I gave them both a kiss on the cheek and headed upstairs to get ready for the day.

I wanted to spend a little time praying and thinking about what was happening and what I was going to do, so I decided to go to the park that was next to the church.

As I sat in the park looking at all of God's amazing creations, I began to think about what Dad had told me this morning. I thought about what had happened over the last several months of my life. As I sat there praying, I felt a sense of calm, and I knew exactly what I was going to do.

Macy had told me that my biological parents had moved to a house that was twenty minutes from where our church was. I really wanted to encourage my biological parents to come to church, and I prayed they could have a better life for my sister. I knew that God wanted this to be a witnessing opportunity for me to try and reach my biological parents. I would get tested and use this opportunity to share God's love with them. After I made my decision, I sat there just amazed at what God had done in my life.

"Rose."

I turned, startled, when I heard someone came up behind me.

"Oh, hi, you scared me," I blurted out as I stood up.

"I went to your house, but you weren't home, so I was headed to the church."

"Sorry, Sarah, I just had some thinking to do, so I started walking and ended up here."

"That's okay. I was headed to the church to meet Garrett for lunch and was wondering if you wanted to come?"

"Sure, I would love to."

I did not realize that it was already lunchtime.

Saturday came quickly, and the time had come for me to go to the hospital to get tested. Mom was taking me because she had to sign a consent form because she was my legal guardian.

As we walked into the hospital, an overwhelming feeling hit me, and then it all went away as I heard these words in my head, "Show others the love that God has shown you." It reminded me that we should treat people in ways that show them God's love, even if we do not think they deserve it.

They brought me to a room and explained what they were testing for, and after they drew my blood, the doctor came in to explain to me and Mom what the procedure would be if I was a match and decided to continue with the procedure.

"Rose, this means even if you are a match, you do not have to go through with it," Dr. Ruttel said after he was done explaining everything.

"I understand, Dr. Ruttel." I reassured him.

"When can she call for the results, Doctor?" Mom asked as we gathered our things to leave.

"Give us a call Monday afternoon."

He smiled and held the door open for us.

"I will. Thank you for everything," I replied, shaking his hand, then we turned and left.

"How are you doing with all of this, Rose?" Mom asked as we headed home.

"I am doing pretty good, Mom. I feel like this is what God wants me to do."

"I am so proud of you, Rose."

Mom surprised me because no one had ever told me they were proud of me.

"Thanks, Mom."

I smiled.

Saturday went by quickly even though I just sat at home by myself. It was time for church, and I was nervous because I wanted to tell Garrett about yesterday, but I was scared of what he would think. I was going through a risky surgery for people who didn't even want me. I tried not thinking about it as I ate breakfast and got ready, but it was all I could think about.

"Hi, Rose," Garrett and Sarah welcomed me as I walked into the youth room.

"Hi, guys, I need to talk to you both. I wanted to be the one to tell you this before word gets out."

"What is it? What's wrong?" Sarah expressed with worry in her voice.

"Nothing is wrong exactly," I responded.

"Then what is going on?" Sarah quickly snapped.

"I need to explain something first."

I went into detail about my sister and her dad's health problems until she knew what Garrett knew.

"So I decided to get tested, and if I am a match, I am going through with the surgery," I explained.

"What? Why would you do that, Rose?" Sarah said, shocked.

"I feel that God wants me to use this opportunity to witness to my biological parents and my sister. I want to show them the love that God has shown me."

"I am so proud of you."

Garrett squeezed my hand and gave me his heart-melting smile.

"I am glad you are using this experience to witness to them," Sarah said, giving me a hug.

"Thank you both. We should get to class."

We walked into the youth class just in time.

After church, I went to lunch with Garrett and Sarah to pass the time and try not to think about the results.

Monday afternoon had arrived, and it was time to call the hospital for my results.

"Thank you for calling Intrest Hospital. May I help you?"

"Yes, I need to talk to Dr. Ruttle, please."

"One moment."

A long pause went by.

"This is Dr. Ruttle. How may I help you?"

"Hi, this is Rose Thomas, and I need to get some test results, please."

"Oh, hi, Rose, let me grab them. Okay, here they are. It looks like you are a match for the surgery. I would like to set up an appointment this week to discuss the surgery more and help you make your decision."

"Okay, how about Wednesday?"

"Wednesday is good. Just come in about nine o'clock in the morning, and we can talk."

"Thank you, Doctor. I will see you Wednesday."

Because Mom and Dad both worked, I decided to ask Garrett to go with me to the hospital to meet with Dr. Ruttle.

"Are you nervous?" Garrett asked as we started to enter the hospital.

"A little, but I still feel this is what God wants me to do," I replied.

"I will support you in any decision you make."

Garrett grabbed my hand, and we entered the hospital.

"Okay, Rose, here is the information and paperwork to take to your parents if you decide to do the surgery," Dr. Ruttel explained as we started to sit down in his office. "Are there any questions you have for me?" he continued.

"I have a few questions."

We went back and forth asking and answering questions for over an hour.

When we finished, Dr. Ruttel shook our hands and said, "Okay, go home, talk it over with your parents, and let me know."

"Great. Thanks for all your help."

I smiled and turned to leave the room.

"Oh, and, Rose, not to pressure you, but if you are going to do it, the sooner, the better. He is going downhill fast," the doctor added.

"Thank you."

I was glad the doctor told me.

"Rose, its Macy. How are you?" the voice on the other end of the phone said enthusiastically.

"Hi, Macy! I'm good, and you?"

"I'm good. I was calling to see if you had decided whether or not you were going to take the test."

"I have made a decision, but before I tell you, I would like to meet with you and your parents to talk."

"Okay, Dad cannot get out, but do you want to come here Saturday? We could have lunch."

Macy was so excited.

"Yes, that will be fine, I think. I will ask my parents, and if they don't mind, I will be there."

"Wow. Your parents? That sounds weird, but okay. See you Saturday."

Saturday, I woke up and got ready to go over to Macy's. My parent's agreed to let me go only if I took someone with me, so Garrett was going.

"Hunny, call us if you need anything," Dad said as I gathered my purse and keys.

"I will. I am going to pick up Garrett, and then we will head over there."

I gave them a hug and hurried to my car. I was so nervous. Having Garrett with me would hopefully help.

As I pulled into Garrett's driveway, I noticed he was sitting outside on his steps, waiting for me. He climbed in, and off we went. The drive over was very relaxing. We talked about everything other than the surgery, and it was great. When we pulled up to the house, I took a deep breath, and up to the door we went.

As I knocked on the door, the nervousness was growing.

"Hello, Rose, and you must be Garrett. It is nice to meet you. I'm Amy."

"Hi, Amy, it is nice to meet you as well," Garrett said politely.

"Hi, Amy, may we come in?" I had never called my biological parents by their names before. It felt like they were real people again.

"Yes, please, Brian and Macy are in the living room."

Amy led us to join them.

"Hi, Rose!"

Macy jumped up and gave me a big hug.

"Hi, Macy," I replied, returning the hug.

"Would you like to eat lunch? It is ready."

Amy helped Brian up and guided him to the table as we followed.

After lunch, we all sat in the living room to talk.

"Rose, I just want to say I understand if you do not want to be a part of this. We did not give you any reason to want to help me," Brian said softly and weakly.

"Your right, Brian. You did not give me any reason to help you. However, God gave me a reason. God showed me love and forgave me of all my sins. God says, 'Show others the love that I have shown you.' I want to show you the love that God has shown me. I have already taken the test, and I am a match. I have talked to my parents, and I am going through with the surgery," I explained.

"I don't know what to say."

Amy sniffed.

"How can we ever repay you?" Brian asked as a tear rolled down his cheek.

"You do not have to repay me. I just ask that when you feel better, you all join us for church on Sundays so that you too might learn of God's love," I extended the invitation.

"We have seen something has changed you. We will think about it," Amy replied.

"I am so excited you are going to help my dad. I hope we can get to know each other better also."

Macy smiled.

"Me too. I will call the hospital first thing Monday." Smiling, I stood up and turned to Garrett. "We should probably get going."

"Yes, we should," he agreed.

"It was very nice to meet you all," Garrett said as he shook their hands.

* * * * *

"Hi, Rose, it's Dr. Ruttel. I am calling to let you know we have scheduled the surgery for Thursday at nine o'clock in the morning. Does this work for you?"

"Yes, Doctor, I will be there."

"Okay, great. You will need to be here at six o'clock in the morning to be prepped, and do not eat anything after midnight."

"Okay, thank you. I will be there."

Wednesday evening, Garrett offered to take me out to dinner for the last good meal for a while. He took me to a very fancy restaurant that I had never even heard of before. As we were sitting there, talking, Garrett began talking about the future.

"Rose, how many children do you want?"

"Um, I don't know, two. I would love to also be a foster parent after my kids are a little older. How about you?" I answered, feeling a little weird talking about it.

"I think it is awesome that you want to be a foster parent," he replied. "So if you could have any kind of wedding that you wanted, what would you have?" he asked with a mischievous grin.

"Well, I have always dreamed of having a Christmas wedding." I went on and on about every last detail.

After I finished talking, I looked into his eyes, and he was mesmerized. I began wondering if he was thinking about us getting married or just trying to distract me so I wouldn't think about tomorrow's surgery. Either way, tomorrow's surgery was the last thing I was thinking of. I could only think about why Garrett was asking questions about marriage and children. I had not thought about it before, but thinking about it, I could see myself marrying Garrett and even having children with him. I would like to graduate high school before getting married though.

"So are you ready for tomorrow?"

Garrett smiled as he walked me to the door.

"I am ready to get it over with. I am glad God gave me this opportunity, but I am nervous and want to be done with it."

I sat on the steps of my house as I finished.

"I trust God will be with both of you tomorrow. Can we pray?"

Garrett took my hand as he began to pray.

When he finished, he said, "I love you, Rose, and I am so happy God put you in my life. I will meet you at the hospital in the morning."

Garrett looked into my eyes and brushed the hair off my face before giving me a passionate kiss.

"I love you too, Garrett. I will see you in the morning."

I was so emotional because this was the first time we said that we loved each other.

I went to bed with an array of emotions. I was so happy Garrett said those three words, and I was also scared for tomorrow's surgery. I knew that God would be with me, and that helped me fall asleep.

The next morning was early. I had to be at the hospital at 6 a.m., so I set my alarm for 4:30 a.m. We left the house at 5:30 a.m. and entered the hospital at 5:50 a.m. Garrett was already there along with Amy and Macy. They were sitting in the waiting room, waiting for us to arrive. We greeted one another and sat down.

"Rose, we are ready for you."

A nurse entered and took me to a room.

* * * * *

"Everything went great. We are observing both of them for a few days before they can go home. You guys can go in and visit. Remember, they are both still out of it a little," the doctor announced after the surgeries were complete.

I stayed in the hospital for four days, and Garrett was by my side the whole time.

* * * * *

It was time for me to go home, and because Mom and Dad went back to work this week, Garrett offered to pick me up and take me home. While in recovery, all I could think about was the talk Garrett and I had the night before my surgery. I wondered if he felt the same way about me as I did for him. I was still sore but glad to be going home.

Over a month had passed since the surgery, and I had not heard one word from Amy, Brian, or Macy. I did not regret for one minute what I did. I knew God used this experience as a witnessing tool not only for my biological parents but also for others who heard the story. I could not wait to see what God had in store for my life and the life of those around me.

ABOUT THE AUTHOR

Jenniffer Clark is a wife and mother. She grew up in Northeast Oklahoma where she still resides with her husband and teenage daughter. Jenniffer obtained her master's in psychology with an emphasis in child and adolescent development and is currently working on her PhD in psychology. She has worked with children and adolescents for over twenty years. Her experience includes day cares, home visitation programs, and school settings. Jenniffer loves spending time with family, whether it is watching her daughter cheer or having family movie night. She enjoys writing and using her God-given talents to help others.

Printed in the USA
CPSIA information can be obtained
at www.ICGtesting.com
LVHW091446120424
777240LV00031B/385